A Science Fiction Novel by
Pat McAnulty

The
Beginning

Book One of the
Exodus Trilogy

International Digital Book Publishing Industries

IDBPI & the Digital Book logo are trademarks belonging to the
International Digital Book Publishing Industries.

Book design & cover by Johanna M Bolton

PRINTED IN THE
UNITED STATES OF AMERICA

First Edition

WCD 10 9 8 7 6 5 4 3 2 1

THE BEGINNING
A novel by the up and coming new writer,
Pat McAnulty

Approximately 66 million years ago a great meteor hit Earth destroying 75% of all life on the planet. For the 25% of animals that managed to survive, life was precariously balanced for another million years.

Now it was happening <u>AGAIN</u>!

In 2019, a meteor destroyed San Francisco killing thousands, and initiating some dangerous ecological changes. Scrambling to understand the cause, scientists discovered that more meteors were coming. They estimated that the next and more devastating hit on Earth would be in the year 2058.

The only way humankind could survive was to find a way to leave their home world and spread into the galaxy. They had some time to prepare, but not much.

This is the story of the brave men and women who saved mankind. It's the story of Sally Richards and Joe Cooper, whose efforts after the 2019 disaster won them the Medal of Freedom, and an invitation to join the newly revitalized NASA. Together they set off with the first wave of galactic pioneers to start settlements on the Moon. But the second wave of pioneers had to go much further … to Mars and beyond. Could they be ready in time?

This book is dedicated to

Ruben Colon

My mentor and writing coach.

He will be missed …

THE BEGINNING
Book One

CHAPTER 1
The Beginning

Saturday, October 28, 2019 8:00 a.m. Day 1

Sally raced from the kitchen of her Upper West-Side, New York apartment, clicking off her cell phone. Shaking and with sweaty fingers she fumbled for the remote on the ottoman in the living room. The flat screen flicked on, and the headlines reiterated along the bottom of the screen:

At least two million people dead in a massive meteorite impact directly on the city of San Francisco. Shockwaves expanded as far as Sacramento. A mushroom cloud filled with debris and steam rose in the clear, daybreak sky up as high as 40,000 feet. Tsunami watches have been issued as far as Hawaii. Waves over 50 feet flooded surrounding areas.

With mouth open and eyes welling, Sally watched a reporter turn his mike to a young man in his twenties.

"Please give us your name, and tell us why you are here."

"My name is Tom Johnson. I live about a mile from here on the north side of San José. The first thing I heard was a low rumble that kept getting louder and louder. I looked up and saw a ball of fire streaking across the sky. It went north. Of course, I didn't know what it was. And then a boom thundered that made the biggest explosives on the Fourth of July sound like firecrackers! My dog ran under the front porch. I'm lucky I didn't wet my feet, if you know what I mean."

"Did you have any idea that a meteor hit San Francisco?"

"Heck no. It seemed like the explosion hit over the ridge of my property. I thought World War III had begun. It scared me so much my hands are still shaking."

"Thank you, Tom. And now back to you in the studio, Rose."

Sally dried her cheeks with a tissue, listening in disbelief as the details unfolded. There had been no time to flee. No time to warn anyone.

Or so they said. College student and amateur astronomer, Jimmy Wharton, had seen a small, undocumented object through the telescope at the local university two nights before while searching the skies over Littleton, California. He reported his discovery to his astronomy professor, who dismissed the information in disbelief.

And then Sally thought of her cousin Jeannie in Denver. Wasn't she going to San Francisco this week? She was an editor for *Sheek*, a ladies' fashion magazine and planned a layout meeting for a future issue she needed to go over. Oh my God. It was this week. Sally picked up her cell phone and called Ben, Jeannie's husband.

"Hello?"

"Hey, Ben... Is Jeannie in San Francisco?"

"Yes. But she is coming back today. Why?"

"Oh, Ben. Oh, no." Her hand slapped over her mouth.

"What is it Sally?"

"You haven't heard. San Francisco is devastated! Turn on your television."

"What do you mean, devastated?" And then Sally could hear the TV in the background. "Oh my God! Oh my God! I don't believe it. Sally, I've got to go. I'll try to get Jeannie on her cell phone. I'll call you right back." The phone went silent.

There was nothing to do but wait. And continue to watch the news.

The tests she graded and the manuscript she penned lay forgotten on the kitchen table. With the call from her mother, the world had changed.

After ten minutes, the phone rang again, and the Caller Id indicated it was Ben.

"Hello, Ben, what did you find out?"

"She didn't answer her cell phone, Sally. My stomach is in knots."

"I know. So is mine. Maybe you could call the airline. I'm sure she got out of there."

"I called the airline, but the lines are busy and I couldn't get through."

"Oh, Ben. I don't know what to say. I'm sure she's OK."

"Well, I'll keep calling the airline and we'll have to wait and see. Sally, I don't know what I'll do without her."

"Don't talk like that. I know she's all right."

"I have to go and try to find something out. I'll call you back if I hear anything."

"O.K. You take care."

"Bye."

Sally held the receiver in her hand clicking it off. She snailed her way across the room and knelt on the bay window seat. Hands cupped under her chin and elbows settled on the sill, her eyes welled again as the view blurred. Jeannie. She couldn't wrap her head around the fact her favorite cousin might be gone. They were like sisters.

The tranquility of the Hudson River offered no comfort as she tried to absorb the magnitude of today's events. Poor Ben. Married only five months, the glow of matrimony still enveloped the couple whenever she visited them. Jeannie made such a beautiful bride. Was it possible she perished?

Her mind regressed to two months earlier when Steve Harding broke their own wedding engagement and moved to Houston to be a physician for the NASA Space Program. Still hurting and angry, she winced at the recollection of their hope and joy when they dropped their NASA applications into the mailbox the day after graduating from Harvard. They celebrated over dinner when he received his appointment.

She heard nothing from the space agency. And her anticipation dwindled as she settled into her position as professor in the psychology department at Columbia University. Graduating summa cum laude with a doctorate in psychology, her ambition in life still sought a bid to astronaut status in the National Space Program. In Cambridge, Steve and she went to the gym and pool, working out constantly, getting into the kind of condition necessary to pass the physical exam of the astronaut program. They studied together until the wee hours of the morning, most nights. But, now, she taught classes and did research at Columbia, while Steve donned a spacesuit at the Johnson Space Center in Houston.

Jealousy gripped her. But that was all water under the bridge. And people admired her, didn't they? Number one in her class. Class president. Main speaker at the National Organization for Psychologists' convention. She had quite a résumé.

Even if NASA didn't think so.

Startled, she turned away from the window and grabbed the ringing phone.

CHAPTER 2
Dan's Mission

Saturday October 28, 2019 9:00 a.m. Day 1

Dan drove like a maniac. At least Kristen thought so. What did it matter if he resembled a Greek god? Tall, black hair and chiseled features, she still could not stand him behind the wheel.

"Slow down! You're going to get us both killed! I don't care if your car is the coolest machine on four wheels." The highway was empty this time of morning and he didn't see any need to watch his speedometer. "You're going to get another ticket!"

"Oh, Kris, calm down. There's no one out here but us. It's good to run an old Porsche wide open once in a while. Besides, I have an in with city hall, even if I am stopped." He did let up a little on the gas pedal for her sake.

Kristen checked her make-up in the car mirror.

"Yes. You are beautiful." Dan remarked.

"Oh, stop, and watch the road."

She turned on the XM satellite radio to get her mind off his driving. Flicking through the stations, she stopped on the national news.

Two million or more killed instantly and the city is devastated... Her mouth fell open, as the news unfolded about San Francisco. Emergency management teams are being summoned from all over the country.

Dan slowed down to the posted speed limit. He was equally stunned. His father, the Governor of Texas, would no doubt be summoned to an emergency meeting to see what could be done to help.

"Perhaps I should go back to the house. You can come too. Who knows what this might mean? We might even get involved. They will probably be looking for volunteers to help with the recovery. This just might be what I need to launch my career. Anyway, there might be something we can do."

Dan decelerated and turned his signal on. He pulled into a driveway and then looked around as he backed up and turned the wheel to go the other way. As he headed back toward the Governor's mansion he once again broke the speed limit. Only this time Kristen kept silent. They turned into the wide pillared entranceway.

A guard bent over and studied the two occupants. Recognizing them, he pressed a button and waved them on. The twenty-foot tall gates opened and the cherry red, 911 Porsche sped up the driveway. The stately Governor's home towered three stories high in front of them. Giant pillars ran along the front of the house, and winding steps led down to the circular driveway. Dan's suite occupied two rooms on the third floor. Having been told of her son's arrival, his mother stood near the front door. Kris followed Dan up the steps to meet the petite, blond woman waiting on the landing.

"Oh, darling, I am so glad you came back home! Have you heard the news?"

"Yes, Mother, that's why we're here."

"Your father is in the library. Perhaps you should go and see him before he goes to the office. Kristen, why don't you join me for a cup of tea?"

***

Dan jogged across the rotunda, passed the elevator, and easily bounded up the massive circular marble staircase to his father's library and study where he spent every morning before he went to work. Approaching the double doors, he lifted his hand and knocked.

"Come in!" announced the older man.

Dan turned the knob of the solid, mahogany doors and entered into a room lined with law and historical books stretching along every wall from floor to ceiling. The décor spelled masculine, with its over-sized, leather sofa and chairs, and feudal oak accessory furniture completing the room. Behind a nine-foot long, desk dominating the far end of the library, sat a portly man, reading. The son walked across the room and casually plunked down on a plush, dark red chair.

"Hello, Dad."

Governor Alexander lifted his head, dropped the newspaper, and immediately stood. Circling the desk, the tall man sat down in the chair next to Dan.

"I am so glad you are here, son. What a catastrophe in San Francisco. I have a meeting in an hour with the emergency management group. The government will be sending troops to the area out there to keep the peace and try to prevent looting. You can't get within twenty miles of the city. The meteorite made a direct hit. The Golden Gate Bridge is gone. The city is gone. The people are gone. What a disaster!"

"Dad, I want to go there. I could be an emissary for you. It would be good for our aspirations, and I want to help."

"We might be able to arrange for you to assist in some capacity. I really don't want you to go because of the danger, but it may have political advantages. You've had a lot of negative press, lately. It appears the cosmological danger is over. You could go in my place. Let me talk to a few people and your mother. Pack your bags."

CHAPTER 3
Joe Cooper

Saturday, October 28, 2019 9:30 a.m. Day 1

The alarm rang and Joe reached a drooping arm over the bed and slapped at the clock a couple times trying to hit the snooze button. He had a class to teach, even though it was Saturday. Being the junior professor, he could never get the good schedules. He had been on the faculty for two years after leaving the rat race of the corporate world.

While at Middletex Industries, he excelled at research of oxygenetics and filtration, and worked endless hours on his invention, the Robux Filter. When the economy collapsed, the government grant money dried up. The company downsized, and he was offered a severance package. Joe declined, and negotiated to buy the patent of his project filter, instead. Now, as a professor at UCLA, he enjoyed summers off to work on and perfect his beloved filter. He built an addition on to his garage and spent all of his spare time and money there. If he could just have one more summer, he knew the Robux Filter business would take off. A thousand facemasks made with his filter were stored in a small ware-house waiting for a volcano to erupt or some other catastrophe to occur that would need his filter…

He rolled over and kissed his wife gently on the cheek. She let out a low moan and turned away from him. She must still be upset. They had a fight the night before about him applying to NASA, and she still hadn't forgiven him. What was the matter with her? The party was especially for him. He received the Hensen Science Achievement Award for his work using quantum physics. They were talking Nobel physics prize for crying out loud! She should be proud of him. Why had their anniversary fallen on the same day? And he had forgotten. So Anna had left the party without him. How many more spats would it take before she had had enough? She threatened to leave him many times. Especially lately.

As he shaved, he looked in the mirror. The image reflected a man of thirty-one, whose muscles, a result of going to the gym three times a week, were well-formed on his slim six-foot-three frame. Girls seemed to like his facial features. Black hair. Green eyes. They all said he looked like Brad Pitt, the movie star. But Anna said looks weren't enough for her. She didn't understand the time it took to make a business succeed. And now, applying to NASA to be in the space program seemed to push her over the edge.

He poured himself a cup of coffee and turned on the television. He always watched the local news before he went to class. But today the local news was preempted with the catastrophe in San Francisco. So that's what the noise was he heard that stirred him a couple of hours before the alarm went off. After watching in disbelief for a few minutes, he wrote a short note to post on his door at the university. He dressed quickly and left. The note read:

"Dr. Cooper's Physics 302 class is canceled indefinitely."

"Joe. Hold up a minute. I've been trying to reach you. Could you come to my office in the Faculty Building? I need to talk to you right away."

"Sure," said Joe. He was a little surprised Dean Jones knew what he looked like, given that the man had only spoken to him a couple of times. The first time was when he was hired. And the second was at the Christmas party. Joe kicked up a few fallen leaves as they passed by the dry fountain in the middle of the park, and crossed the street. They climbed the steps to the second floor and entered the dean's office. The Dean motioned him to sit down on a chair in front of the oak desk.

"We are all in a state of shock," Joe's boss said and without giving Joe a chance to comment he went on. "I received a call from Washington an hour ago. You may get to try out your new filter mask near San Francisco. Homeland Security would like you to go up there to test and monitor the air quality, and try out the mask they spent so much money on. And they want to buy all you have in stock and can manufacture in a hurry."

Joe's mind raced. This could be my big break. I have spent years perfecting a mask, easy to put on, sealing the face, and still allowing in oxygen. I own the patent, but the market has proved minimal. The Afghanistan War has worn itself out, and the troops are home. A few miners use the mask, with great success, but the sales have never climbed enough to let me quit my "day job" being a professor.

"When do you want me to go?" Joe inquired.

"As soon as you can be ready. We'll have a police escort waiting for you at your house. A truck will pick up the masks. It's about a three and a half-hour drive to Fresno. You'll spend the night. Here's where you will stay." He handed Joe a packet. "At twelve thirty, tomorrow, you'll pick up a woman at the Fresno airport. She's from New York. Her name is Sally Richards."

"You mean THE Sally Richards, who has written books, lectures, and teaches psychology at Columbia University in New York City?"

"She's the one. Here is a sign to hold up at the airport so she will know you're her escort."

On the way home, he thought about Miss Richards and realized he had never actually seen her. She had lectured at his university on the effects of trauma to people in catastrophes, but since it wasn't his field, he didn't go. But he listened to her lecture on the campus radio. He pulled into the driveway. There in front of his house waited the police car and truck.

Joe pushed the garage door opener and drove his Silverado into his side of the double bay. Anna's car was still there. Strange, he thought. Anna usually had left for work by this time. As he walked into the house he could hear muffled laughter coming from his bedroom. He followed the sounds and when he got to their room, there laid Anna, in bed. She was not alone. His friend Frank sat next to her. Joe, stunned, walked over to his closet and pulled out his suitcase without saying a word. He threw clothes into it and slammed it closed.

"Joe. What can I say? Anna choked.

"Don't say anything," said Joe. It took him five minutes and he departed out the door for the last time.

CHAPTER 4
Sally's New Direction

Saturday October 28, 2019 5:30 p.m. Day 1

Sally sat on the bed in disbelief and, again, stared at the Hudson River out her window. Jeannie must be dead. Although it was getting dark, she didn't think to turn on the light. Ben called and told her that Jeannie did not make her flight. So, she must have still been in San Francisco when the meteor crushed the beautiful city. Poor Ben. He had choked out the horrible news.

Until an hour ago Sally had been glued in front of the television. But now she gazed as dusk fell, at the quarter moon glowing near the horizon. The lights of the city came on one by one. After the moon disappeared over the horizon, she moved to get up. The phone chimed, once again.

"Hello?"

"Hello. Is this Sally Richards?"

"Yes, it is."

"This is George Constable from FEMA. I am sure you have heard about San Francisco."

"Yes, of course."

"Sally, we need you to go to California. You have the most expertise in the area of psychological trauma in the United States. Many survivors in the surrounding areas, as well as the rescuers, are struggling. Many will develop post-traumatic stress disorders. We have cleared it with Columbia University, and you are to be given a leave of absence for as long as it takes to do your job. If you are willing to go, all your expenses will be paid, and you will be on the government payroll for the duration of your stay. What do you say?"

"You know, I was half expecting a call from someone like you. Of course, I will go. Just tell me when I need to be ready."

"Tomorrow morning a military escort will pick you up at five thirty and take you to La Guardia airport. There, a helicopter will fly you to McGuire Air Force Base in Wrightstown, New Jersey. You will board a C-17 that is taking other military personnel and supplies to Fresno, which is as near as a plane can get to the impact area. Pack work clothes. You won't need anything fancy."

"Don't worry. I'm not a fancy person. How much clothing should I take?"

"Just pack for a few days. The rest you can buy when you get out there."

"I'll be ready."

Sally hung up the phone, and immediately called her boss from Columbia.

"Hi, Steve. I'm sorry to bother you at home, but I received a call a few minutes ago from a George Constable from FEMA. Do know about this?"

"Yes, Sally. FEMA wanted the best Psychologist in the country and, of course, your name came up."

"I'm flattered. Do I need to cancel my lectures, or has that been taken care of?"

"It's all arranged. All you need to do is get packing."

"O.K. Thanks, Dave, I'll keep in touch. Bye."

After tossing the cell phone on the bed, Sally went to her closet wondering what the next chapter in her life would bring.

CHAPTER 5
Sally Meets Joe

Sunday, October 29, 2019 6:30 a.m. Day 2

The next morning, Sally watched out the window of her apartment for the government vehicle. Casually dressed in khaki pants and jacket, she figured she would leave the plane and go immediately to a staging area.

The flight proved uneventful. After dozing and reading for four hours and thirty minutes, they landed at Yosemite International Airport in Fresno. The airborne dust clouds made it impossible to fly any closer to ground zero.

Deplaning down the steps of the huge airplane, she spotted a man on the tarmac holding up a sign with her name on it. She walked over to him.

"Sally Richards?" asked the man as she approached him.

"Yes, that would be me."

"Welcome to Fresno. My name is Joe Cooper." He cleared his throat as he gazed at his new acquaintance. She was tall, about his age, and not the matronly figure he imagined. He continued, "This airport is about as close to the impact event an airplane can get. There is still too much fine fallout for planes to fly to San José. The dust could make a turbine engine fail. We will be taking a Humvee to the staging area. Not too fancy, but the military found out in Iraq they do well on dusty roads."

They walked into the terminal building and started down the concourse. Sally followed him as they weaved their way around the other travelers and military call-ups. Her dark auburn hair suddenly blew wispy tendrils around her face as Joe opened one of the front doors. Joe didn't think her gorgeous, but a lot prettier than he expected.

They had no trouble identifying their transportation. It looked like a flattened jeep, but bigger. The camouflage paint scheme blended with an army lieutenant's uniform as he stood leaning up against it with arms folded. When the soldier saw the couple, he hurried over to them.

"Let me take those," he said reaching for their suitcases on wheels.

Joe handed their bags over to the lieutenant and watched his fellow passenger bend over to enter the vehicle exposing a well-formed derrière.

Joe raised his eyebrows at the soldier. The soldier nodded in agreement.

Sally settled herself on to the seat, and turned her head to look out the side window. The airport had lines of taxis picking up people who had flown in to search for loved ones. Some were red-eyed with dried tears. Others were waving down taxis. None were smiling.

Pulling away from the curb, the lieutenant gave short blows to a siren to move the traffic in front of him. He slowly maneuvered his way to the less congested exit road. They made their way through town to Route 99 and headed north.

Their destination was San José, a little over two hours away. That was in normal times. Now, there were roadblocks on all the highways leading to San Francisco. The officer told Joe and Sally it would take a long time before they arrived in San José.

When they were on open highway, Joe turned to the girl sharing the bench seat and said, "So, tell me about yourself. You must be pretty important to have your own military escort." He smiled.

"Well, this is a pretty unusual situation. To tell you the truth, I had no idea who would meet me at the airport. I just knew that he or she would probably be holding up a sign. If no one would have been there I would have had to make a few phone calls."

For the first time Sally studied the other passenger. He appeared to be in his late twenties or early thirties. She thought him attractive with green eyes and black hair. It passed through her mind that he was half a head taller than her own figure. She always seemed to make a note of that with men, since she stood almost six-feet. Her belly rolled as she thought that Steve had been as tall and appealing as this Joe.

"Are you from New York?" asked the handsome escort.

"Yes. I grew up in Manhattan. Big city girl. But you wouldn't know it by looking at me, today. I graduated from Harvard and earned my doctorate there. Now, I'm a professor of psychology at Columbia University. I will head the group of doctors who specialize in helping survivors and families deal with their grief."

Joe looked into Sally's eyes. "I don't know how people can have a job like yours."

Understanding and compassion showed on her face. "It's difficult. But I can't imagine doing anything else." After a moment of silence, she continued, "Where are you from?"

"I came up from Los Angeles, yesterday. I also teach, but at UCLA. I am a research scientist in the field of quantum physics. I used to work in the rat race of the corporate world, but it didn't take long for me to decide it wasn't for me. He didn't mention his dreams about working for NASA.

"Are you married?" Sally inquired. She asked the driver to lower the visor to keep the hazy sun out of her eyes.

"No." lied Joe. He wanted to leave all doors open. His heart still ached about the scene at his house the day before. But he had decided then and there that he and his wife were through. Thank God, they didn't have any children. He continued, "Are you?"

Sally stared at the computer between the seats as she answered, "No." She hadn't spoken a word about Steve Harding to anyone since they broke up two months ago.

The traffic started getting heavier. The soldier didn't speed. He weaved in and out of traffic as other drivers slowed down to let him pass. Sally now realized why a military escort was necessary to get her to the command center. She was getting tired and closed her eyes. She didn't know how long she had dozed off when the siren of the Humvee blared, startling her. Her green eyes flew open and she was astounded by what she saw. It looked like winter outside the vehicle. Snow-like dust was everywhere. They were at a roadblock and the driver was trying to get around jammed up cars. Troopers with masks covering their faces were checking the I.D.s of the few cars in line trying to pass through. They had reached the barrier where only a few people were allowed to go any farther. As soon as the men saw the official orders they were motioned through.

After a few more minutes they stopped in front of a modern, gray office building. An eerie orange sun reflected off the massive black-looking windows making Sally squint. A sign as they entered through the gates read: Fairfield Industries. They passed through a tree-lined circular drive and stopped at the front door.

"Here you are, sir, said the Lieutenant. I will wait out here until you return."

"This is where we get out." He reached around to the back seat and pulled two masks out of a pouch. "Put this on," he said handing her one of them. He donned the other one himself. "This is my invention. It will trap the dust. Soon everyone will be wearing them. They are much lighter and efficient than the gas masks worn by the soldiers. The shipment from my warehouse should arrive today. The military made thousands of them before they ended my project."

He opened the door and quickly skirted the vehicle to the other side to open Sally's door. Footprints in the dust marked his path. Opening the car door, he took her hand and she got out. "Welcome to San Jose´. Sorry, but it doesn't usually look this way."

Mask donned, she observed the still landscape. There appeared to be little destruction except for the dust.

As they approached the front double doors, a stoic sergeant opened them and they walked in. "Are you Sally Richards?" Before she could answer the soldier turned to Joe. "Are you Dr. Cooper?"

"Yes, we are," they said in unison.

"Then please follow me."

Inside, Sally noticed the entryway opened to a large rotunda. Modern in design, the walls echoed and her low heels clicked as they walked along the marble floor.

Removing their masks, they were led down a corridor and stopped in front of one of the many closed doors. The somber escort knocked.

"Come in," a male voice said from within.

The guard opened the door. Joe and Sally entered a grand luxurious office. The tapping sound of their feet ended as they stepped onto a thick red carpet. Sally looked around. Pictures on the walls looked like originals. She was sure one was a Picasso.

"Please. Take a seat." He motioned to them to sit in matching brown leather chairs in front of a solid mahogany desk. "I trust that your trip here was uneventful." He went on before they could reply. "My name is John Wheaton. I am Director of FEMA. We are using this complex as a staging ground. Mr. Fairfield was kind enough to let us use his personal office to organize this mission. I am relocating to the triage area, tonight. Let's get right down to business, shall we? It is my job to supervise the entire operation. We will continue to search for and rescue survivors. While this is going on, we will put out fires and stabilize the area around the crater. We will determine the amount of damage the meteorite has caused as well as determine its effect on the environment. Doctor Richards, you will organize a relief effort to manage the psychological needs of the survivors and rescue teams. As you saw outside, everything is covered with a powdery dust."

He nodded to Joe. "We will be using the masks you have designed and completed for the next few days, or until you report that the air is clear enough to breathe without one. You will be responsible for making sure that the filters are being used properly and take care of any problems that may arise. I understand that you have used nano-technology to create them. Fascinating. The rest of FEMA's leaders will be here tomorrow. There will be people with a variety of expertise to be part of our group. Some will be scientists like you. Others will be politicians and reporters."

Mr. Wheaton turned to Sally. "Joe will be your co-worker. He will be with you most of the time. We have paired people to account for each other until their established at the triage." He turned to Joe." Your equipment will be delivered tomorrow. In the meantime, I suggest you get some rest. I'm sure you have had a long day. You'll stay at the Marriott downtown. Lieutenant Parker will take you there. Please. Have dinner, get settled, and then I suggest you get a good night's rest. I will meet you here tomorrow morning at eight a.m." Finished, he stood and added. "Do you have any *Quest*ions?"

Sally rose and replied, "No. But I'm sure I might have some as soon as I leave this office." John Wheaton appeared a little stressed and to the point. She would reserve her opinion of him until another meeting.

"How about you, Doctor Cooper? Any *Quest*ions?"

"No sir." Taking Mr. Wheaton's cue, he rose and together they headed for the door.

Joe let out a sigh and handed Sally one of the masks as he said "Well, that's it. We can go." He led Sally outside, his hand under her elbow. They bent over and stepped into the Humvee. When they were on their way, it seemed like they had to stop every five minutes at a barricade to present their orders.

They were not alone on the road. National Guard troops could be seen in the back of trucks as they headed in the opposite direction to the devastation. Rigs with bulldozers and other equipment sounded their horns as they passed slower vehicles. Red Cross trucks raced by them. Sally turned and peered out the other window. The only physical sign of a meteorite was the white soot that covered everything. They were many miles from ground zero and the rim of destruction. Houses and automobiles, trees and shrubs had become a winter wonderland. Sally thought it resembled a Currier and Ives post card. Here, buildings were intact. But only the military could be seen walking around. Local residents were told to remain inside until they could get masks. Sally saw a few cows and horses. They were nuzzling the ground to push the dust aside eat the grass.

Finally, after an hour and a half, they reached the hotel. In the lobby a few people milled, mostly reporters. Their dressy attire and the camera-clad men who stood near them was a dead giveaway. One reported, using a live feed, as Sally headed toward the front desk to check in. Joe carried a small duffle bag and waited his turn behind Sally.

Signed in, Joe asked "Are you hungry?"

Sally hadn't even thought about it until now, but she felt famished. "Yes. I'm starving."

Off the lobby, a restaurant with lights on appeared to be open.

"How about we take our belongings up to our rooms and meet down here in ten minutes?"

"That sounds good." They entered the elevator encased in glass. Arriving at their floor, they found their rooms were only a few doors apart.

"See you down in the restaurant in a few minutes," Sally said as she slid her card into the holder unlocking her door. She unpacked her few belongings, freshened up, and headed back downstairs.

The restaurant was almost empty. A waiter led Sally to her table. She sat down and the man asked if she would like something from the bar. She studied the wine list and said "Riesling, please."

The man returned carrying a crystal glass. As he set it down, Sally lifted her head and asked, "Why are the hotel personnel still here? I mean, I would think that you would be gone like everyone else."

"We were ordered to stay by the military, so we could take care of people like you...not that I mind." The man's sad eyes studied the table as he lowered his head and continued, "I live, or I should say lived, in a house fifteen miles north of here near Palo Alto. I don't know if it's still standing. I don't have insurance. But I feel lucky. Nobody was home at the time. June, that's my wife, works nights at an all-night diner, downtown. My kids were with me on the Bayshore Freeway on our way here. I take them to school at 6:30 a.m. They go to a Christian school near Santa Clara. Tammy's five, and Nathan's seven. We heard and felt the blast, but by God's grace, we all survived. I talked to June at the diner and she was all right. She came here, to the hotel, before some of the roads were blocked. I didn't see much other damage, and the dust hadn't settled, yet. My family's in rooms upstairs. The manager said we can stay here until things settle down." He smirked as he pointed outside. "Literally. Well, I'd better get back to work. There are lots of reporters, military, and rescue workers to feed. Do you know the Governor of Texas? His son is here."

She noticed on his shirt pocket his I.D. Tag displayed the name, Robert. "Thank you, Robert. I'm glad your family is safe."

Her drink lay half empty on the table as Joe walked into the room. He had changed from a suit to a casual outfit of khaki pants and a blue polo shirt. His hair looked damp from a shower and was spiked in the front. White teeth caught her eye as he smiled and said hello. I believe that is a dimple in his chin, she thought.

As he sat down he said, "Sorry I'm late. But I decided I really needed to get cleaned up. I had dust everywhere." He ordered a beer and asked the waiter for menus.

"We aren't using them," Robert said. "All we have is soup and some sandwiches. The supply trucks couldn't get through, and we have very little vegetables and meat."

After ordering, Sally realized she still wore the clothes that she had on since she left New York and felt frumpy. But at least she had brushed her teeth and quickly recombed her hair. Oh well.

"So what made you decide to be a scientist?" Sally asked.

"Sometimes I ask the same *Quest*ion. I have a degree in mechanical engineering and a doctorate in physics and bio-chemistry. I started my career as an inventor in the corporate world. The rat race and throat squeezing wasn't for me. I know it sounds like a cliché, but I wanted to invent some-thing that would benefit mankind and make a difference. I ended up teaching at UCLA and working summers to market my Robux Filter. I've invented an oxygen and gas mask us-ing quantum physics that I think is better than anything on the planet. I received a call that the government wants to use the ones already manufactured. I'm here to supervise their use and monitor their effectiveness. You wore one earlier. You probably saw that it's much lighter, smaller and less restricting than the ancient ones the government has been using since the Vietnam War. The filter can also be used on air intakes of all kinds of engines."

Sally, fascinated, asked, "How does it work?"

Joe went on. "Well, little particles called nano-chompers eat the dust. There are billions of them in one fil-ter."

She laughed. "Eww! Don't tell me I had bugs in my mask!

"In a way, you did. If it is a success, maybe NASA will take notice."

Sally's mouth flew open. "I don't believe it! NASA is where I want to work! I've had my re´sume´ on their desk for two years. I'm still waiting."

A look of dread showed on Joe's face. Then he stammered, "I...I let that slip. Please don't say anything. If UCLA finds found out, I would be out of my day job."

"Don't worry. I would be fired at Columbia University if they heard what I just told you."

He hesitated and went on, "I guess you're right. It'll be our secret. Going to NASA has always been a passion of mine. But in today's political and economic climate, I'm afraid I'll never get hired there."

"It's been a passion of mine, too! I'm a professor of psychology at Columbia University right now, but my real desire is to fly to Mars and other celestial bodies to study the effects of limited living quarters on the human psyche. There have been many reservations about sending people for long voyages to other moons, because they may not be compatible with each other for extended periods of time. That's where I'd come in. I'd be responsible to keep the peace. But NASA hasn't, as yet, given me the nod."

Their food came. As they ate their soup, conversation ended. Sally studied the room around her. Reporters and cameramen quietly talked to one another as they, too, waited for their meals. The doorway caught her eye. A group of soldiers dressed in green fatigues entered the room. Their clean clothes gave away their recent arrival. Soon, they, too, would be digging through the rubble for survivors, relieving exhausted local firemen and volunteers and locally summoned National Guard troops. They made their way to tables of their own and more waiters and waitresses took their orders. Tonight they would share warm cozy rooms. But tomorrow their strenuous work would begin.

Again, her eyes were drawn to the entryway. An entourage of people including more reporters rapidly writing and holding recorders up as close as they could to one man's face. She was too far away to hear them, but whoever it was they were following must be important.

"Who could that be?" Sally asked Joe.

"I think I heard the governor's son from Texas is here to give his support, and be an emissary for his dad, but I'm not sure." At that moment, their loquacious waiter came over to their table to give them their bill.

"Excuse me," Joe said, "do you happen to know who that man is over there getting all the attention?"

Robert bent down and said in whispers, "He's the governor of Texas's son, Dan Alexander. Quite the jet setter and playboy. I see him on the news all the time. He dates Kristen Dobbs, the Vice President's daughter. He wants to get into politics. But needs to clean up his act, first, if you know what I mean."

CHAPTER 6
Dan Arrives

Sunday, October 29, 2019 7:00 p.m. Day 2

Dan felt exhausted. His flight, on the private Gulf Stream V, from Texas had been long and bumpy. During the flight he practiced his speeches with the writers and took a short nap. Soon, the pilot made the announcement to prepare for landing in Fresno.

As he peered out the corporate jet window on the tarmac, he couldn't believe that, as usual, the offensive paparazzi had beaten him to the scene. Disgusted inside, he stepped off the plane onto the Fresno ramp waving and smiling. Security made a path for him. And after a few minutes he sat in his waiting limousine. As the cameras flashed, he sank down into the rich tan leather.

He closed his eyes after they had pulled away, and frowned. He poured himself a bourbon he found in a mini-refrigerator in front of him. His thoughts regressed to the scene on the front lawn of the big house. When his family said their good-byes, his mom's eyes welled up as his dad shook his hand. Kristen hugged him like he'd never return. It seemed anytime he left to go anywhere it was a big production. But his Dad just gave him the familiar salute, with no words of encouragement. *I guess I should feel lucky he let me go in his place.*

His entourage filled three limousines. Almost everyone had solemn countenances except Eddie, one of his dad's assistants. It made him sick to watch him. He could tell jokes in a hurricane. *Did you hear the one about this…Did you hear the one about that…*All Dan could think about was what they were going to see tomorrow and how he would come across when he gave the speeches prepared for him by his father's people.

And he was tired. Kristen begged to go along but that proved to be out of the *Quest*ion. The paparazzi would have loved it, but he had had enough of them. And they weren't even formally engaged. It was inappropriate. At least, at this time.

With a police escort, he and the members of his party drove until they reached the Marriott. He opened his eyes when they stopped in front of the hotel, and the driver handed him a mask. A big man, the cop appeared to be of Mexican descent and could easily have doubled as a body guard.

"We need to wear these for now. The military issued these back at road block 24. You were asleep. Must've been a long trip, huh? The back of the mask is fastened with Velcro so you can adjust it the way you need to."

"Thanks," said Dan as he fumbled with the straps. "Did they say how long we have to wear these things?"

"Oh, I think they said for a few days. I don't know if my tolerance will last that long, though," he answered, grinning. He had a full mouth of white teeth with a gold filling right in the front. He opened the door and moved quickly for someone of his build. Opening Dan's door, the Governor's son stepped out and realized his driver must be at least six-foot-seven.

Reporters swarmed around him as he took in the "snowy" scene. White flakes were everywhere. His entourage pulled up behind his limo, and followed him up the steps. Eddie turned around and counted heads and made a mental note that everyone had made it through the barriers.

"Let us through. Let us through," the driver shouted as they made their way into the lobby. He took his mask off as soon as he made it through the swinging door. Dan pulled his over his head and ran his fingers through his hair. Eddie scurried past him and, immediately, went to the front desk to sign them all in. After shaking many hands, several microphones went to his face and the *Quest*ions started flying.

"Did you have a good trip?"

"How long are you going to stay?"

"How close are you going to get to the Impact Event?"

"When are you and Kristen going to get engaged?"

Dan's stomach gave a little twist at the sound of the last *Quest*ion. So, the paparazzi were here, after all. How crude. But he kept smiling and pulled out a prepared brief speech to brief the reporters. He turned to them and spoke.

"Hello everyone. I just arrived from Texas about three hours ago. The Governor wants to issue his sincere condolences to all those whose loved ones, friends and acquaintances lost their lives, are missing or injured in this unprecedented tragedy that occurred yesterday. The state of Texas, as well as all the states of this union, band together to join in your mourning. The President will visit tomorrow at 2:00 P.M. and personally assess the damage. He has called upon all of his resources to join in the search and rescue of those who are still unaccounted for all around the city of San Francisco and the Bay Area. Tomorrow, beginning at 8:00 a.m., I will visit some of the sights and the Woodside Triage, where I will give words of encouragement to all I possibly can who are involved in this enormous disaster. Those with special clearances will join me. It will be your responsibility to record and video the account for us alive today and for posterity. May you do your job, well. Thank you."

With that he stepped away from the flashing cameras and microphones and headed to the sign that read Vanity Restaurant. He was starving.

CHAPTER 7
The Road North

Monday, October 30, 2019 7:00 a.m. Day 3

Sally met Joe in the lobby early the next morning. Men in military uniforms filled the area. News personnel with cameras of all kinds were milling around. A few other civilians could be seen talking to each other and checking in and out at the front desk. Most of the reporters' eyes focused on the elevator. The word escaped that Dan Alexander planned to come down, shortly. Sally noticed the commotion, and as she and Joe followed their gaze, a man in khaki pants and sweatshirt walked up to the couple.

"Doctor Richards. Doctor Cooper?"

"Yes?" they said in unison. They turned around to face a thin middle-aged, mousey man with fading red hair. The man continued.

"My name is Eddie. I am Dan Alexander's assistant during this trip. I work directly for Governor Alexander of

Texas. We are here to help in any way we can. It has been arranged for you to join us, along with a military escort, to see some of the damage first hand, today, and transport you to your duties at the main triage at Woodside.

"Later, we will separate, and you will get started with your mission. The trip will take most of the morning. We have continental breakfasts and coffee for you on the way. Director Wheaton will brief you as to your specific instructions when we're there. We will drop you off at his field command post at 9:00 a.m. You will be in vehicle number three behind Mr. Alexander."

At that moment, the elevator doors opened. The media crowded Dan as he scanned the lobby. When he spotted Eddie talking to the two strangers, he made his way around the flashing cameras. Ahead of him, security guards held people back. He stopped and leaned over his assistant and whispered in his ear that he had a few things to discuss with him before they left. Eddie smiled, excused himself and turned his attention to his temporary boss. While Dan and his aide talked to each other out of the hearing range of Sally and Joe, every few seconds, the Governor's son looked over at them nodding and smiling. When they were finished, Dan crossed the lobby and stopped in front of the couple.

"I'm sorry to be so rude. My name is Dan Alexander. I am a big fan of yours, Miss Richards." He extended his hand, first to Sally and then to Joe. While they took turns being polite, he continued. "Doctor Richards I am so glad to meet you. You were the author of the textbook I used for Psychology in college at Yale. Doctor Cooper, I would love to know more about the masks we have been wearing since I've been here. I understand you invented them."

Sally and Joe were speechless for a few seconds. Sally made the first move. "How would you remember the author of a textbook?"

"My psychology professor was in love with you and mentioned your name during almost every class. Plus, we received extra credit if we went to any of the lectures you gave at Yale. That's when I became a fan. John Wheaton chose well for this mission."

"Say," Dan added. "Why don't we go in the same car and maybe we'll get a chance to talk?" He turned to his assistant. "Arrange it, please, Eddie."

After Eddie performed his magic, six people and the driver filled the shiny, black Chevy Suburban. Dan sat in the front seat. General Morley and his lieutenant-guide sat in the middle two seats. Joe, Sally and Eddie sat in the back. They were all introduced by Eddie, and salutations were quickly made. Leaving San Jose´ on Interstate 280, they headed northwest. Joe noticed the visibility to be about three miles, better than yesterday. The dust was settling and the wind was calm. He estimated they would need to wear their masks outside about four more days as long as the wind stayed light.

The soldiers loaded his equipment into one of the vehicles following them. He would take periodic measurements and test to make sure his masks were working. They didn't need a repeat of 9/11/2001 when so many firemen, rescue workers, and survivors had long-term effects of dust inhalation.

The caravan comprised of a TV truck, four Humvees, two jeeps and three stretch SUVs filled with reporters, cameramen, and dignitaries like Dan. Slowly, it made its way along the Junipero Serra Freeway and through the grey Los Altos Hills. They stopped at many checkpoints.

"Doctor Richards, what made you decide to get into psychology?"

Sally smiled at the governor's son and replied, "I have always cared about people's feelings and what makes them tick. I guess I felt therapy and research would fulfill the desire to help people. Writing, lectures and teaching followed."

"You made my course in psych more enjoyable. I went to a few of your lectures at Yale. My professor adored you and your methods of teaching."

Dan turned his attention to the other scientist. "This is an opportunity for you to see how effective you mask is. It is pretty comfortable considering I hate to have to wear a mask. How does it work?"

"The best way to explain it, I guess, is to tell you small particles, using nanotechnology, collect the dust and dissolves it. The mask's filter lasts about three months with constant use."

Dan raised his eyebrows. "That is really interesting."

Eddie nodded.

Joe asked Dan, "How did you happen to come on this mission?"

"My dad would have liked to come, but urgent business prohibited him, so he asked if I could take his place. Of course, I said I would. I flew in last night on our jet. I promise we did not use taxpayers' money." He smiled and continued, "I want to do everything I can to help comfort the injured by visiting make-shift triages and local hospitals." He didn't say a word about Kristen and nobody asked."

Joe thought of more personal *Quest*ions, but decided this was not the time or place to ask them.

The two military men sat and said nothing.

After passing ten miles northwest of Stanford, the entire landscape changed. The smell of smoke and the bumpy ride diverted Joe's attention from the small talk to the outside. Sickened, he saw some houses crushed and some razed by fire and still smoldering. The others noticed his shocked face and followed his gaze. Their mouths fell open as they saw the roadside median piled with stones and rocks that were scattered everywhere. Some approached the size of boulders. Crews of rescue workers were still trying to extract anything living from the damaged buildings pummeled with showers of falling missiles. The car slowed way down as they passed bulldozers and trucks with cranes carefully removing debris. Emergency vehicles could be seen on the opposite highway rushing the injured to better equipped facilities.

The lieutenant noticed their faces and explained. They listened intently.

"Hopefully," he said, "there may still be survivors. There are tens of thousands of missing people. We had to plow the roadways ahead like snow in winter to get the debris and rocks pushed aside. We've only been able to reach a small number of survivors. We have lost communications with the areas twenty miles or less around the circumference of the crater. We hope to keep plowing the roads. But most are under water. It is expected that in two days with the approval of the military experts and Doctor Joe Cooper, we will be able to fly with rescue helicopters closer to more of the destruction. Up ahead, you will see larger and larger boulders. Most trees are gone and the closer you get to the Impact Event, the land changes from grey to brown where the water has receded. The meteor struck the earth at exactly 6:00 a.m. three days ago on October 27th. By the time our sky watchers discovered it, it arrived. A crater approximately ten miles in diameter was carved by the impact. Debris and steam rose to about 40,000 feet into the atmosphere causing the white dust we see covering everything within a forty-mile radius around ground zero, especially to the southeast of ground zero. The meteor hit directly on the downtown area of San Francisco. The city is gone and in its place is a new bay with a partial rim and a totally new landscape. Water from the Pacific filled the entire area and there is no land where the city proper used to be. Death was instant for those who lost their lives at the impact area. Outside this circle of destruction, a giant wave of water over two-hundred-feet high exploded upwards and outwards and crashed down ten to fifteen miles from the center. Thousands of people were crushed or drowned. The water gushed in a small tsunami outwards to the Pacific and the surrounding valleys, leaving newly formed lakes and mud in its path. Planes cannot safely fly over the crater, and no one has been closer than eighteen miles. It is still too hot and the steam is still cooling. We are getting pictures and video from satellites. The deluge has receded now, but the old and new rivers are still treacherous as the water roars to the newly formed reservoirs. Around here, the water followed the valleys so where it stayed dry, fire was prevalent. As you can see, the dead and injured are being evacuated, and we haven't given up on finding more survivors. We happen to be arriving from the southeast. Of course, the damage is not only at ground zero, but all around the circumference of the crater. There are thousands of rescuers to the north and east of the San Francisco area. But much of the area is flooded including Oakland. We will not be able to go much farther, because about five more miles ahead, we will dip down to a valley that is now a giant bay." The lieutenant stopped and became silent once again. The general did not speak.

****

Sally's eyes slowly turned from the speaker to the dark windows of the large SUV once again. She had only a few other life changing events in her life. Her cousin, Jeannie, was not the first encounter with death. A tear rolled down her cheek as she remembered her mom dying in Sally's tenth year. When I really needed her. Cancer is such a horrible disease. I lost her little by little as the illness crowded out her organs and filled her thin body with out-of-control cells. Finally, after seven months of suffering, Mom died. And I was alone. My dad still lived, but where was he? He didn't even show up at her small funeral. Sally couldn't remember if her mom and dad were officially divorced. He simply didn't show up one day. And that was that. Her aunt took her in, and actually treated her well, but she couldn't take the place of her mom who doted on her and fixed her hair. When nine-years-old, Sally wore braids with pretty ribbons and her mom called her "my beauty." She came to most of her school functions. Especially when she received honors for her scholastic excellence. She breezed through school. Living life proved tough. Until she met Steve Harding. He became her prince charming. He wrote love letters and put them on her desk at the university. But ambition lured him away. He received NASA's letter accepting him into the space program and left. What would she have done? She couldn't blame him. The space program, scaled down, accepted only a select few. She sent her application at the same time he did. But she heard nothing. Yet.

****

Joe glanced at Sally next to him, and noticed her tear-filled eyes staring out the window. He felt for her hand. Her fingers slowly folded over his and she held tight. His mind shifted back to two days ago when he left his home and Anna. It seemed like months ago. He could not go back. His marriage was finished. Nothing he had done in the past warranted her being unfaithful. Why couldn't they have talked it out? Why did it have to be Frank, his best friend? He would see a lawyer when he had the chance. He would start a new

life. Would this woman who held his hand be part of it?
Time would tell.

CHAPTER 8
Dan's Awakening

Monday, October 30, 2019, 9:00 a.m. Day 3

Dan's stomach sickened by what he heard and saw. He sat slightly sideways and glanced back at the three in the back seats. His gaze moved from Sally's clasped hand to her face. Her eyes shifted to his. He gave her a slight smile of understanding. Kristen would have been crying, too, he thought. She cried one day when they ran over a strange cat on the road.

Eddie spoke first. "In twenty minutes we'll make today's stop. It's at the military triage where General Morley will leave us. Lieutenant, you will come with us and answer more of our *Quest*ions. Mr. Alexander, you will have a photo shoot with the other VIPs while you mingle around the troops and give words of encouragement. I'll be with you the whole time to guide you. You'll need to wear your masks outside. Dr. Cooper, I have been on the satellite phone, and you are to monitor your instruments that are in a vehicle behind us. It is my understanding the masks can be worn for long periods of time. I hope so. This will be a true test of your invention, Doctor Cooper." He turned to Sally. Doctor Richards, I am glad to see you seem to be feeling better. You will get your specific orders from John Wheaton, the head of FEMA, who I believe you met at his temporary headquarters in San Jose. He drove up here last night to assess the damage. He will introduce you to the psychologists and psychiatrists who are tending to the survivors and rescuers to help them deal with what they have experienced. Most of them know people who are dead, mutilated or missing. The injured are being transported as soon as they are stable. The mentally affected patients are also transported immediately. It is my understanding that there are only a few roads open leading to the point of 'No Entry.' Triages in this area only go as far north as Redwood City. We can't get to Belmont or any farther north. A lake covers the highway. So, the scene is dismal. You may all see more than you care to. Please try to focus on the jobs you all have to do and the good coming from doing them."

They reached the top of a hill with a sign reading: Woodside two miles.

Sally stared straight ahead out the front of the Suburban. Halfway down to what once was a valley, the interstate disappeared into a huge bay. The vehicles slowed down. Joe noticed they were on an exit ramp. They turned left onto the newly plowed, bumpy road.

Emergency trucks, and other military vehicles passed them headed the other way. The view stretched into a wet wasteland. There was no detail. No lawn chairs on the remaining brick houses. No sheds. No garages. No people. Although there was vegetation, the gray, grassy fields were matted down from the water that flowed and then ebbed back to form the bay. There were rocks everywhere. But no sign of fire. There wasn't much left of the small town. A building resembling a gas station stood on a corner. Foundations where fragile houses had been torn by the wind and water lay like skeletons. Debris laid everywhere. A few trees were left but most of the leaves were gone. A large tent stood in the middle of the town square. A sign in the front showed a red cross. This was the triage for this area and headquarters for the others established around the Impact Event. Troops with masks labored everywhere. Joe noticed before they stopped, that the visibility appeared much better here, maybe ten miles. He would take measurements right away. The group pulled up to the tent and stopped.

"This is where we get out," said the Lieutenant as the convoy stopped. "Everyone, put your masks on."

Reporters and cameramen scurried from the jeeps first. They began snapping pictures of the devastation and rushed to the black SUVs. Dan opened his door and faced the barrage of reporters. Eddie ran around his side of the vehicle and created a barrier between Dan and the media. Without allowing Dan to answer the onrush of *Quest*ions, Eddie led him to a large military tent set up in the middle of the bivouac. It reminded the Governor's son of the circus tents where he had eaten cotton candy and watched the "Greatest Show On Earth" when he was a boy. A guard opened the flap and Dan and his entourage entered into a huge one-room makeshift hospital.

The place bustled with nurses and doctors and other young recruits and reserves. It was difficult to stay out of their way. They circumnavigated boxes marked individually with towels, bandages, Betadine, and many other supplies piled high, making a maze leading them into the midst of the makeshift hospital. Rows and rows of army cots lined the sides, almost all of them occupied with injured bodies bandaged and covered with green and brown blankets and sterile white sheets. The tent smelled of medicinal alcohol and damp earth and groaning could be heard from many cots. They passed plastic-walled areas where simple operations were being performed.

Eddie directed Dan over to a moaning woman, where he took her hand. The cameras flashed. Bandages covered the patient from head to toe. He put a rose into her other hand and leaned down and kissed her on her bandaged cheek. "You're safe now," soothed the governor's son, "and we will take good care of you."

The woman stopped whimpering and looked up at Dan through dull grey eyes.

"Have you found my family?" she whispered.

Dan couldn't help the tears that welled in his own eyes. A drop fell on the hand of the ailing woman. He wiped it off and said, "I'll do everything I can." He stood and moved to the next cot and then the next and the next. When he was done, the media had their shots and Dan knew this day had changed the course of his life.

CHAPTER 9
Executive Orders

Monday, October 30, 2019 11:00 a.m. Day 3

Sally and Joe, led by two corporals, approached a motorhome to the left of the main tent. Sally jumped out of the way to avoid getting splashed by spewing muddy water flung by the wheels of a siren-blaring ambulance as it buzzed by them. Rows of emergency vehicles stood in line to retrieve more of the maimed and dead bodies brought initially to this triage and carried to the hospitals in San Jose´. Rows of smaller tents filled acres of cleared land. These were used for sleeping, communications and preparing food. Port-a-potties were everywhere. "Water buffalos," trucks filled with potable water, parked near the main tent nicknamed the "big top," enabled the troops to bathe and drink. The smell of blended smoke, sea water and wet grass reminded Sally of a campground she stayed at with Jeannie and her aunt and uncle when she was a little girl.

When they reached the 45-foot camper, their escort knocked on the door.

"Come in! Come in! came a boisterous voice from within. A hand reached down to help Sally up the steps. It belonged to John Wheaton.

"I hope your trip up here has been enlightening. I'm sure it has. And Doctor Cooper. How are you? It's quite a mess isn't it? Here, make yourselves comfortable. Take your masks off. Wipe your feet on that bristled mat or feel free to take your shoes off. Dr. Richards, why don't you sit right here on the couch. Joe, you can sit on that recliner behind you. I'm sorry the quarters are so compact. We brought our own Prevost camper because we didn't know how long we were going to have to stay here. I feel guilty since all the military are in tents, but, oh well, rank does have its privileges," he muffled a laugh.

Sally's initial opinion of the head of FEMA changed quickly. Instead of being stuffy, he acted pleasant and kind. She scanned the luxurious recreational vehicle. Advertisements don't do them justice—they are nicer than I thought. And they cost over a million dollars. Mr. Wheaton must be doing very well. Jeannie and I slept in a pup tent.

The FEMA director went on. "Does everyone know each other? Ah, let's see, Sally and Joe, this is my secretary, Penny." He waved his hand over to his assistant, a pretty middle-aged lady with premature white hair. She already had an armful of papers. "Penny, this is the Sally Richards and Joe Cooper I have told you so much about. Behind me, over by the sink, is my wife, Susie. Our little Yorkie, Pebbles, is around here somewhere, probably back on the bed." He turned to the trim, attractive woman wiping off the counter. "Honey, would you get us something to drink?"

And once again, facing the two doctors, Mr. Wheaton continued, "Let's get down to business shall we? We have twenty-two triages set up throughout the recovery area around the Impact Crater. This one, called Woodside, is the headquarters for all the rest. At this time, we can get no closer to the rim, which is twenty miles to our north. Doctor Richards, your job is described in this manila envelope." Penny handed it to her. "It mainly consists of these points: One, organize the work of all the psychological factors in recovery. Two, help the distressed to overcome these factors. Three, limit the publicity relating to these factors. Four, oversee the psychological recovery of the injured and the workers." The FEMA administrator took a packet from his secretary and handed it to Joe. "This one is yours. The instructions inside are self-explanatory. But you will mainly: One, monitor the masks and pollution. Two, monitor all filtering units to the temporary tents Three, supervise any repairs."

The phone rang.

"Hello? Oh, hello, Sir. Just one moment." Mr. Wheaton covered the phone and turned to the two visitors, "I'm going to have to take this one in the other room. It's the President." He rose and went into the bedroom sliding the pocket door shut behind him.

While the FEMA leader talked on the satellite-phone, Sarah thought about Jeannie. Could it be she is lying on a cot injured in one of these triages? But there were so many. But how could it be possible?

About five minutes later, with Pebbles under his arm, Mr. Wheaton came back into the room. "Well, I have great news! The President's coming out here today. He is already on his way. Air force One landed in Fresno three hours ago. He has left San Jose´ via military escort and will be here around noon. That's only two hours from now. A catered luncheon will be brought with him and you are invited. It will be very informal in keeping with the situation. Tables will be set up at one end of the "big top." You know, I wondered why so many military men were here including General Morley who came with you today. He is making a last minute check to make sure the area is secure for the President. As it is, the reporters are already here for the other dignitaries; unfortunately, they will get upstaged when the President is here. Actually, this is the first time that it has been considered safe for him to come. Even though he will have to wear a mask outside, he is thankful for Doctor Cooper's invention that is working so well."

Sally sipped her lime drink and searched through her packet. She raised her head and smiled at Joe. As he smiled back, he dropped a couple of sheets of paper on the carpet. She chuckled. There was something about Joe she liked. Down to earth and, well, warm. Like a comfortable couch.

John Wheaton's phone rang again.

She thought about the President coming. Politics didn't interest her. But she concluded the unpopular President, Jonathan Vail, making the effort at such a dirty and dangerous time to see the devastation firsthand, would boost his ratings. She had never seen him in person. Nor had she voted for him. She could not support a candidate whose platform did not include spending money on a space exploration program.

It took about an hour to read and organize the material that the two had been given to them. They had moved over to the galley area and the dining table to spread their papers out. But now they both were done.

Joe raised his head. "Well, I'm ready. Let's get started."

"Me too," said Sally. She cleared the table by carefully putting all the papers back into her packet.

Mr. Wheaton nodded to them as they donned their masks and headed for the door.

"See you in the big tent at 1:00 o'clock," he called to them, holding one hand over the phone.

"I have to find a Doctor York," initiated Sally as they stepped outside. "He will introduce me to my crew here at Woodside. What do you have to do?"

"I'll be on my own until lunch taking readings and checking supplies. I must check for any failures."

"Well, I'll see you later, Joe. Good-luck."

"Yes, you too."

They both about-faced and walked in opposite directions. After a few steps something made Sally turn and look around. At the same moment Joe's head turned back and their eyes met. Joe slipped and almost went down into the mud. Sally muffled a laugh in spite of the situation, shook her head and headed toward the "big top."

Maybe I will get a second chance…

CHAPTER 10
The President Visits

Monday, October 30, 2019 1:00 p.m. Day 3

"Welcome, Mr. President," announced John Wheaton. "I'm sorry to have to see you again under such circumstances. Please come right this way."

The tall slim man stepped out of his black limousine into the hazy particle-filled air wearing his filtered mask. The Commander in Chief, surprised how well he could hear and understand his masked FEMA director, anticipated meeting the inventor who made it possible to enter this area safely at this time. Thousands of people were being rescued because of the Robux Filter. The two VIPs made their way toward the main tent while cameras flashed and secret servicemen scrambled. Once inside, the heavy flaps closed and the masks came off. The President ran his fingers through his hair. His face somber, he immediately said he wanted to see the injured. A general led him to the right, around makeshift walls, until he came to the same area that Dan had visited two hours before him. Beds stretched for rows upon rows and were all filled with wounded people of all ages. Some were awake and some were unconscious or drugged to ease the pain. Most were waiting to be transported to hospitals. Some, not yet stable, lay in total psychological distress with eyes staring into space.

The President went from bed to bed and wiped the brows of many men and held the hands of many weeping women. His sleeves were rolled up and he made no speeches. "Let them make up their own speeches this time," he said later when asked by his press secretary why he hadn't taken advantage of such a golden opportunity. It was after 2:00 p.m. before he came to the end of the rows of wounded individuals. And at lunch, he could not eat his own meal. But he shook hands and talked with the workers, helping morale.

Sally and Joe sat at one of the long tables eating their boxed sandwiches hoping they would get a glimpse of President Vail. Dan Alexander gave an interview at the end of the long table. The two professors were almost finished when a commotion could be heard coming toward them. The couple glanced at each other and Joe winked at her. Sure enough, around the corner came the President and his entourage. And one of them was John Wheaton. As soon as John saw Joe he walked straight over to him.

"Joe. I would like to introduce you to President Vail. He is thankful for your invention of the Robux Filtration System that has enabled us to come this close to the crater and save all these lives. He is very grateful." Joe stood immediately and extended his hand. He was trembling. In his wildest dreams he hadn't anticipated this.

"It's an honor, Mr. President." He couldn't think of another thing to say.

"Sometime when this is all over, you'll have to come to the White House and explain it all to me."

Joe's mouth dropped. "I would be glad to, Mr. President." he replied, his face turning white.

John Wheaton turned to Sally. "And President Vail, this is Doctor Sally Richards, a professor of Psychological Studies at Columbia University. She is my assistant, and head of psychological trauma for the people in all the devastated areas during this crisis.

"It is my honor to meet you, Doctor Richards," said the Commander in Chief. We are grateful for the time and effort you are giving toward this unprecedented cause."

"Thank you, Mr.President."

The President glanced down the table and happened to see the governor's son. He nodded to Sally and Joe, and hurried past every one toward the man. "Dan. Dan. How are you?"

Interview over, Dan stood and said, "I'm fine, Mr. President, how are you?"

The President remembered where he was and added, "I am sorry we have to meet in these circumstances, but it is good to see you. Give your dad my regards."

"I will."

A secret serviceman noticed the time on his watch and nodded to another man who gently took the elbow of the President. The Commander-in-Chief followed the staff member toward the exit. Soon, he was gone and the press hovered back over to Dan and a few other dignitaries.

CHAPTER 11
Danger!

Monday, October 30, 2019 2:30 p.m. Day 3

"So, what do you have to do this afternoon before we leave?" Sally asked Joe.

"I have to check a Robux unit feeding one of the tents. It's not filtering properly. What's on your agenda?"

"I am going to categorize patients into groups. This way we know where to send them by the severity of their symptoms. So, my psychiatrists and psychologists will be very busy. I guess I won't see you until on the way home at 5:00 P.M.

Sally spent the time after lunch accomplishing her tasks. She divided the available doctors into teams and assigned to them patients and traumatized recovery workers. So far, there were fifteen professionals. More were on their way from other parts of the country and would arrive tomorrow. Their instructions awaited them including transportation to

take them to their assigned triage unit. They would then report back to her with statistics, problems, and other needs.

Most of the media departed when the President left.
Dan held scheduled interviews with reporters from television
networks, taking three hours. He held a private meeting with
John Wheaton in the director's motorhome.

At five o'clock, tired and hungry, the Governor's son
dropped into the front seat of the Suburban. Joe and Sally
ducked their heads climbing in behind him. Eddie typed on
his laptop in the rear seat and worked without glancing up.
The rest of Dan's entourage left a half hour ahead of him. As
the sun sank below the horizon, it cast shadows over the car.
Nobody talked to each other as the hefty driver turned out of
the muddy driveway onto Interstate 280 and headed south
toward San José. Sally put her head against the headrest and
closed her eyes.

They drove for thirty minutes when Sally sat up
straight.

"What was that?" she said. "Is our tire going flat?" She
could feel a rumbling sensation coming from under the car.

Dan said, "I think we ran over some debris."

"Maybe it's another meteor!" Eddie yelled, as the jig-
gling got worse.

The driver stopped the vehicle. The shaking intensified.

"It's an earthquake!" Joe shouted to everyone as he put
his arms around Sally. "Hold on!"

Eddie's papers fell on the floor. Sally started praying.
The car bounced like a ping pong ball. Eddie yelped when he
hit his head on the ceiling. He did not wear his seatbelt. Sally
knew they were skidding over the pavement each time they
landed, and wondered how much concrete remained. The
SUV kept moving until finally, the wheels thumped as each
one went over the edge of the road. It kept going. Suddenly,
she heard crashing and cracking that sounded like thunder.

The car fell on its side as it slid bumping into a deep black ditch that seemed to swallow them up. And then all movement stopped.

****

Sally lay conscious but confused. Joe's arms had just been around her, but now her body covered his with legs and arms every which way. Darkness had fallen, and the headlights produced an eerie glow while providing some light within the vehicle. She didn't feel hurt and attempted to move.

Joe spoke first. "Are you all right?"

"I think so."

"Can you roll over? I'd like to get up if I can move. You're kind of heavy, and my arm is twisted."

Sally heard groans coming from somewhere else. She couldn't see the others because the seats were in the way.

What seemed like minutes, but was just a few seconds, Joe called, "Is everyone, O K?" They heard whimpering.

"Is that you, Eddie?" Joe asked as he tried to right himself. Sally rolled to the right, and realized she sat on the rear door of the vehicle. The SUV moved a little. Joe grabbed the back of the seat.

"Where are we?" Dan's assistant implored.

"Are you all right, Eddie?"

"Oh, I'm not sure. Where is everybody?"

Joe creased his brow. "What do you mean?"

"There's nobody in the front seat!" screeched Eddie.

As Joe and Sally untangled themselves from each other, Sally reached over the seat and pulled herself up. Eddie was right. The bucket seats in the front were empty. And the right front door hung open. They heard a faint groan.

"Help me." Came a voice from below. "Down here. Under the car. It looks like Mr. Alexander is hurt real bad."

Sally knew the deep voice belonged to the driver. She tried to look out the window under her. It was pitch dark and she could not see anything. Joe stood up and reached for the left door. With a labored push, it opened. He stepped on the arm of the seat and climbed his way through the orifice and on to the "new" roof. With the light from the headlights, he could see ground and jumped. The Suburban creaked. He told Sally to stay put until he took a look.

The situation appeared bleak. Joe walked around the Suburban cursing the dark, and back to the open door.

"Hey Eddie. Look in the console area or glovebox to see if you can find a flashlight."

After a few seconds, Eddie returned with one and flicked it on. Thankful, Joe took it and hurried to the front of the vehicle to peer down over the edge. The crack appeared to be about a three and a half feet wide fissure made by the earthquake. He couldn't determine the depth. By the voices it seemed to be about twenty feet. And then more fear shot through him as he realized the car was wedged precariously down in the crack on its side at an angle of about seventy degrees. If another tremor undulated, the Suburban could crash down on the two people stuck in the hole and the two left inside would also be seriously hurt.

"What are we going to do?" Sally stood next to Joe.

Visible, thanks to the headlights, Joe reprimanded, "You don't listen very well."

Eddie also climbed out of the SUV and said, "We're not wearing our masks."

Joe could barely make out the small man by the tree.

"Tonight, it's priorities. Sally, go back and take a quick look, without getting back into the car, and see if there are masks handy. If not, forget about it. They can deal with our lungs later. Right now, I need to get down in that hole." Sally knew all about priorities. Being a doctor presented priorities, often. She would get the masks if possible.

Joe turned back to the two men below him. He cupped his hands around his mouth and called, "Hey, down there. Are you able to move from under the Suburban?"

"I did, Doctor Cooper," called the burly man, "but it's Mr. Alexander that I'm worried about. I tried to move him but his legs are under a boulder that is too heavy for me to move. He moaned, but he's not making a sound, now. I think he's out. And he's right under the car, sir. Is it going to fall on top of him? If we have another earthquake, is this hole going to close up? The sides are like walls, straight up and down."

"Not if I can help it," soothed Joe. He hoped he sounded more confident than he felt.

Sally found three masks and another flashlight. The three persons above the ground could wear them until they reached the injured men down below. When she found Joe walking along the fissure flashing his light at the jagged rocks, she gave one mask to him, and turned and ran back. She put one on Eddie. He was in mild shock, but he appeared stable. Priorities. She put the third one on herself.

Using her newly acquired flashlight, she scanned the hole in the opposite direction from Joe. After about fifty feet, she found what she was looking for. The side of the bank had caved in, and rocks of gradual size created steps down to the bottom about thirty feet down. It would not be easy. One bad move and she could break an ankle or get her foot caught in a crack. She yelled to Joe. He came running.

The distraught driver shouted, "Please hurry!"

"Stay where you are, and we'll come to you and give you some light." Joe encouraged.

"You might know there'd be no moon or stars out. Must be clouds. Maybe it's going to rain," said the driver.

That's all we need is rain tonight, thought Sally. The rocks would be slippery.

Just then, the ground began to dance again. "Oh no! said Eddie. They all fell to the ground until it stopped. It only lasted about four seconds.

The Suburban shuddered and groaned, but didn't move. Bits of rock crumbled down the crevice.

"An aftershock, said Joe. "There could be more. Hurry, Sally, I need to get down in this hole, now! Please hold this flashlight for me."

"Your hands will be free if you hold it in your mouth." Sally replied. "I'm coming with you!"

He did not argue. They started down the rocks. About half way down, Sally thought she had made the wrong decision as she slipped and sat on her butt. The terrain proved steep and her mouth was getting sore having the light in it for so long. Drool dribbled down her chin. Her hands were bruised. But her mind thought about the injured man at the bottom of this crevice.

Finally, they reached the jagged floor. Stones in all shapes and sizes lay everywhere. The bottom appeared treacherous. They climbed over and around the rocks until they reached the driver.

"Am I glad you're here!" said the big man. "I think that I broke my arm in the fall. It aches like a toothache, and pain shoots through it when I move."

Sally quickly examined the man with her flashlight. No blood. Other than his arm, he appeared to be all right. She waved the light all around her.

"Where is Mr. Alexander?" she asked.

"Behind me about fifteen to twenty steps."

Both flashlights pointed in that direction. Sally pointed hers up, and there the six-passenger vehicle sat precariously wedged into the cracked earth. Immediately, she aimed the light back down to the bottom, and there, crumpled, lay Dan, unconscious… or dead.

With trepidation, the three weaved their way to the injured man. Joe reached him first. The Suburban creaked again. The sound came from directly above them.

After putting his mask on Dan, Joe handed his light to Sally and said "Shine them both on this boulder." The big stone appeared to be about two feet in diameter and lay on top of Dan's legs. Blood soaked through his Armani pants and painted the dirt dark red.

"We have to get this off of him!"

The two men grunted, as they tried to lift and push the boulder away from the governor's son. The huge driver could not budge the rock with one arm, but with Joe's help, they inched it off the body of the stricken man and it rolled with a loud thud to the side of him.

Joe frantically racked his brain to retrieve the first aid knowledge he acquired earning his Eagle Scout status many years before. Blood. Lots of blood. Tourniquet. I need to use a tourniquet to stop the bleeding or he'll die right here.

"Do either of you have something to make a tourniquet?" He flashed his light from Sally to the driver.

"Yes," the driver blurted. I have a clean handkerchief."

"Give it to me, quick!" Joe grabbed the extended hanky, and quickly tied it around Dan's lacerated left leg. The other one appeared crushed, but he didn't see any external bleeding.

"Maybe this will slow the flow." Joe half mumbled to himself. And then added, "It doesn't look good. He's pale and unconscious."

"Shhh," said Sally. "I hear something!" They all raised their heads and listened. "I think it is vehicles on the road!"

Just then a search light flashed above them. After a few seconds it flashed again and stopped.

"We're getting help!"

CHAPTER 12
Rescued

Monday, October 30, 2019 7:00 p.m. Day 3

The lights from the fire truck blinded Sally as she climbed up the ladder and out of the crevice, with the help of the firemen. Rescue workers lowered a board to retrieve Dan Alexander from the hole while others secured the Suburban to keep it from falling. At least twenty National Guard's men tended to them.

Sally sat on the ground while she sipped a cup of coffee. A medic taped a bandage to her forehead. Joe walked over to her.

"How are you doing?" he asked.

"Fine. And you?"

"I've been talking to the lieutenant over there." He pointed to a man giving orders. "He says Mr. Alexander is alive, although he's lost a lot of blood. They'll rush him south in the ambulance. They may even try to get a helicopter to intercept him along the way. The air quality is improving fast. We're going to get a ride back to the Marriott Hotel. The earthquake measured 6.2 on the Richter scale and did a lot of damage. We happened to be traveling over the epicenter. We're right over the San Andreas Fault-line. I guess we're lucky to be alive."

"Where are the driver and Eddie?"

Joe scanned the lit-up area. "I don't know. I think Eddie rode in Dan's ambulance."

"How did they find us? Has anyone said?" inquired Sally.

"Sure. The story is, when the earthquake hit, tremors rumbled through the Woodside Triage, although damage was minimal. John Wheaton found out using a satellite phone, the epicenter lay beneath this area. Calculating we were near here and could have been injured, he ordered emergency equipment discharged to this part of I-280. Dan is lucky to get help so soon, although he's critically injured. He's lost a lot of blood. His right leg is mangled and he's unconscious."

They turned their heads to watch the ambulance carrying Dan Alexander pull quickly away, with red lights flashing, but without the siren blaring.

Out of the shadows the military doctor, with a "Major Clinton" patch on his jacket, and the one they saw treating Dan, approached. "Are you Doctor Richards and Doctor Cooper?"

"Yes," they said in unison to the Major.

"Come with me, please. We have a ride to San Jose´ waiting for you. Are all your medical release papers signed?"

"Yes," they replied again together. Joe put out his hand to Sally. With his help she stood, and they moved with the Major toward a military vehicle about thirty feet away.

About half the distance to the Humvee, Sally stopped suddenly and put an arm out to stop Joe.

"Wait! What about our important papers giving us our orders? They're still in the Suburban. We need them."

"We removed everything that we could see, and put it all in the truck we're transporting you in, so don't worry," replied the Major. "Of course, you'll have to organize it all. Papers were strewn everywhere."

In the vehicle, and moving south down the highway, Sally leaned her head back on the pillows provided and closed her eyes. Her mind drifted as they slowly made their way back to the Marriott. Visions of Dan Alexander, pale and lifeless under the boulder, haunted her. How badly was he hurt? Would he live?

CHAPTER 13
The Next Morning

Tuesday, October 31, 2019, 7:00 a.m. Day 4

"Good morning." Sally sat down in a chair across from Joe in the dining room of the Marriott. "Did you get any sleep?"

The scientist stopped typing on his i-Pad and raised his head. He rose briefly as his cohort took her seat, and then sat back down— again. "I slept fine, considering. My elbow is a little sore, but only bruised. How about you?"

"Yes, you could say I am scraped up some. But the worst thing is, I'm hungry. I haven't eaten since our luncheon, yesterday. Have you had breakfast?"

He opened his mouth to answer when Robert, the talkative waiter from yesterday, set water glasses down in front of them.

"Good morning," the pleasant man said as he stood by the table. "I'm sure glad to see you made it back O.K., last night. The earthquake did quite a bit of damage, the troops have been telling me. As if the meteorite didn't do enough." He rolled his eyes. "Can I get you some coffee?"

"That would be great. Thank you, Robert. Did you experience anything from the earthquake down here?" Sally inquired.

"Yes. It started with a low rumbling sound that kept growing louder. The hotel vibrated. Then I heard a loud cracking sound. The building stopped shaking and the rumbling dissipated. It lasted about five seconds. But I haven't heard that it caused any injuries or damage in this area. Servicemen are saying houses and other structures, already weakened by the concussion from the meteorite, collapsed. They don't know how many casualties were involved. Everyone is talking about the rescue of you two and Dan Alexander. You are all over the news. How is Mr. Alexander, do you know?"

"Hopefully, we'll find out today. We made it back here about 1:00 a.m. He's in intensive care at Good Samaritan Hospital. Joe and I are fine, except for a few bruises. We didn't see much, being dark, but the roads appeared to be clear and undamaged. Robert continued. "I heard the Governor of Texas, Mr. Alexander's father, his wife and girlfriend, Kristen, flew out here last night. Well, I'd better get your coffee. The dining room is filling up and I might get fired." He winked.

Sally turned back to Joe. "Are you catching up on reports from yesterday?"

"Ya. I can't find the ones I did at the triage before we left. I brought them with me thinking I could work on them in my room last night. It's amazing how quickly things can change."

"They could be in my stuff. The rescue guy gave me a pile of papers I haven't gone through, yet. I planned to do that on the way to Woodside, today."

"Don't worry about it. I'm almost finished with a duplicate. I can't wait to take new readings of the atmosphere today. I'm hoping we'll only need our masks on outside, a couple of more days. The effects of the impact event weren't as bad as it could have been. The water surrounding the Bay Area minimized the particles that exploded into the air. I think aircraft will soon be able to approach ground zero. I would love to fly to the crater area and take readings. The surface around the center is still too hot for ground personnel to approach the rim."

Sally nodded in agreement. "I'm anxious to get back to the triage sight and begin my work. I believe the media frenzy is calming down. I don't see as many reporters here, as there were yesterday. Although several stopped me on the way in here and wanted my story of the earthquake. I told them, I would talk later. They've been told to leave us alone in the restaurant."

"Ya, they approached me, also. Our moment of fame."

****

After breakfast, Sally and Joe exited the dining room into the lobby and were immediately surrounded by reporters. They answered their *Quest*ions for about ten minutes. Security escorted them to the elevator. When Sally pushed the button for their floor, she said, "I need about five minutes, and I'll meet you back down in the lobby, if that's O.K.? I need to get the papers."

Joe looked at his watch. "Sounds good. I talked to our driver, and he is already waiting downstairs." He glanced up. "Please, don't let there be any more aftershocks on the way back."

CHAPTER 14
Dan's Distress

Tuesday, October 31, 2019 7:00 a.m. Day 4

Kristen's eyes widened as she entered Dan's private intensive-care hospital room. The security guard closed the door behind her. Walking between the injured man's parents, she slowly approached the bed of the unconscious man. Fear wrenched her stomach, overcome with the visual input of life- support machines with their tubes leading in and out of Dan's battered body. The slow rhythmic thump of the breathing machine disturbed the silence in the room. Blood thundered in the membranes of Kristen's terrified brain. Would he live? He couldn't die. They had too much to live for. Our future seemed as bright as a bursting supernova. And now, a mere day later, it appeared as dark and void as a black hole, crushing all their dreams into oblivion.

The Governor and Mrs. Alexander stared down at their son. Kristen circled around to the other side of the bed. She picked up his limp hand and kissed it. Moments passed. No one spoke.

Disturbing the verbal silence, the surgeon, who spent five hours in the operating room trying to save Dan's legs, opened the door and entered the room. "My name is Doctor Steve Maury. I performed Dan's surgery last night. May I have a word with you?"

They all turned to the doctor and nodded.

Leading them to a small private room reserved for V.I.P.s, they followed and the doctor closed the door. "Please sit down." He waited until they were seated and continued. "Dan's surgery went well, but we could not save his right leg. It was totally crushed by the boulder. He has lost a great deal of blood and is very weak, but the blood replenished by the military medical rescue unit and the tourniquet saved his life. His left leg is broken in two places but should mend nicely. His other bruises are minimal. It will be a few days before he can be transported back to Texas to recover there. We need to monitor his vital signs, to be sure there aren't any complications from his leg being crushed. He should wake up in a few hours."

Handing the Governor a card, he continued, "If you need anything, just call me. That card has my private cell-phone number on it. If you want to put out a press release, let me know. I'd be glad to do it. Do you have any *Quest*ions?"

The Governor spoke, "Yes, we need to say something to the media, before rumors run rampant. My press manager will get in touch with you, if that's all right."

"Of course. Well, if that's it, I have another scheduled surgery." He extended his hand, quickly shook hands with each one of them, and left.

****

Kristen thumbed her way through a magazine as she sat by Dan's bedside. His mom and dad had left the room, momentarily, to get some coffee. Nurses came and went, taking his vitals and checking his lines. They wheeled another machine into the room, but didn't hook it up to anything. They said something about his kidneys, but she couldn't hear everything they said.

She noted the time on her watch. Three hours and he had made no movement. Glancing out the window, she observed news trucks lining the street below, with their antennas extended.

About to stand up to stretch, she heard a low moan. Magazine tossed aside, she rushed to his bed and stared at the handsome man who she had been dating for two years. Gauze and tape covered the breathing tube in his throat masking the lower part of his face. What will he think when he finds out he needs an artificial leg? Tears came to her eyes. Thankful he was alive, she loved him enough it didn't matter to her that he had lost a limb. He could still hold office when he decided to run, and she would stay right by his side all the way to the White House. They would stick to the plan worked out by leaders in the field of politics. The injury wouldn't stop her from becoming First Lady.

Dan's hand moved up to his face and back down to his side. He began to regain consciousness.

Kristen took his hand in hers while her heart beat faster. It felt cold. His eyes slowly fluttered open and closed as though trying to focus.

A nurse entered the room and spoke, startling Kristen.

"Looks like our patient is waking up." She adjusted the intravenous lines and monitored the screens above his bed.

"Mr. Alexander, are you cold? Nod your head up and down if yes, and back and forth if no." Dan nodded.

"Can you squeeze my finger?" The patient squeezed. "We will remove the intubation tube from your mouth, shortly," she said to Dan as she pointed to his throat. He nodded, again. "The nurse-anesthetist will remove it. She'll be here soon."

The nurse spread another blanket on him. She turned to Kristen and said, "It's common for patients to be cold after surgery. He may also be thirsty, but his I.V. will take care of his needs. I'll check back in a few minutes. My name is Laura. I am the head nurse for this shift. If you have any *Quest*ions or need anything, I'll be at the nurses' station." With that, she smiled and headed for the door. She passed Dan's parents, as they entered the room.

Eva, his mother, went quickly to the bed when she saw his eyes open.

"He's awake," Kristen said. "But he can only answer yes or no *Quest*ions by moving his head, since he still has that breathing thing in his mouth. I wish they'd hurry up and take it out."

Eva put her hand on his brow and spoke, "Hi, darling. Do you know where you are? You're in the hospital. There was a bad earthquake and you fell into a hole. You've been in the operating room most of the night. They drove you to Los Altos and then life-flighted you to this hospital, in San Jose´. The pilots risked their lives to get you here." Dan stared at the ceiling. She continued, "Hopefully, they'll take that breathing tube out of your throat pretty soon."

Kristen moved out of the way, so Governor Alexander could get closer to the bedside. "How are you doing, son?" said the big man as he bit his lip. "We'll get you out of here in no time. I like our own doctors we have in Texas."

Dan moved his eyes from one person to the next. Kristen wondered what he was thinking. Could he be in pain? How long before the nurses came and removed the plastic tube from his throat? It looked creepy.

Kristen got her wish. Another doctor on duty, entered the room with the nurse and asked to stand by Dan. "Please wait outside for a few minutes and we'll remove the breathing tube. Maybe, then he'll talk to you, although he may be a little hoarse and groggy."

After ten minutes, the nurse told the anxious visitors they could reenter the room.

Dan, now tubeless and more alert, inquired in a whisper, "How long have I been in this bed?"

"Since last night. Do you remember, anything?" inquired his mom.

"Only that we were riding along and the car started bouncing and shaking. I must have grabbed the door handle because the door flew open and I remember falling. But that's it. How is everyone else? Where's Eddie? I hurt all over, especially my legs."

His mom's eyes welled up as she turned to her husband and back to her son.

"Honey, your legs were crushed by a huge rock. One is broken in two places. The other... the doctors spent most of the night trying to save it, but they couldn't." Her tears fell on Dan's hand.

Dan stared, once again, at the ceiling. "Are you saying I only have one leg?"

"Yes," his dad iterated. "The doctors did everything they could to save it, but a boulder crushed it, Eddie told us. The driver, with a broken arm, and another man, a Joe Cooper, pushed it off of you and were trying to save you when the rescue trucks came. Eddie has a few bruises. He's downstairs handling the media. Everyone else is O.K., I think. We need to do something for them, later. But for now, we need to get you healthy again."

"What about my career? What about everything I've been planning for?"

"It won't change a thing. You can be fitted with a prosthetic leg. People have run marathons with artificial limbs. You will still be able to run for office."

Dan lowered his eyes and focused on Kristen.

Kristen tried to read his eyes. How would their prearranged future be different?

CHAPTER 15
Back to Woodside

Wednesday, November 1, 2019 7:00 a.m. Day 5

Joe and Sally's ride back to the triage outpost proved uneventful, although they feared aftershocks. The fissure, opened by the earthquake, gaped visible along the road as they passed by. The Suburban was gone. Chills slithered down Sally's spine when she imagined the mishap could have been more lethal. Headlines written by the reporters said Dan lost one leg, but would survive. The doctors worried he might have symptoms from "crush syndrome" resulting from the long length of time his legs were compressed. She would like to have visited him at the hospital, but security was heavy around him, and he occupied a room in the Intensive Care Unit. Only select people were allowed into his area. Especially, a celebrity. She'd try to get permission through John Wheaton's connections, if possible.

In the meantime, she had much work to do. As they made their way to the site, Joe's gentle snore caught her attention and made her smile. He appeared younger the thirty-two years he said he was, with his eyes closed and lips parted. Deep in her abdomen she felt a butterfly twinge, but vowed she would not attempt another relationship so soon after her break-up with Steve Harding. The demise of her engagement still hurt too much to expose her feelings to another man. He does look awfully cute, though. She closed her eyes to divert her thoughts on the mission ahead of her.

****

Sally delved into her work in the designated area of the "big top." Thirty-three professionals including psychologists and psychiatrists, received their instructions from her. National Guard members set up scheduled sessions with patients who were unable to cope with the traumas they had experienced. Many had lost family members. She thought about Jeannie and felt their pain. Ben kept her informed clinging to the belief she might still be alive. But that seemed impossible. After going from bed to bed, she concluded her cousin wasn't here. She checked with the records keeper and found nothing. Afterwards, she took a deep breath and returned to the job at hand.

"Miss Richards?" A fireman entered her makeshift area. They provided her with a desk, behind which she sat and read reports.

"Yes?"

"Do you have someone I can talk to? I haven't slept in four days and I'm exhausted."

"Haven't you had a chance to rest?"

"I can't. When I lie down and begin to fall asleep, I start to dream that I'm being sucked into a huge crater filled with water and I'm drowning. People are yelling for me to help them, but I can't."

"What is your name?"

"I'm Bill Tate."

"Bill, I'll have someone prescribe something that will help you to rest peacefully tonight. Then, I'd like you to make an appointment with Dr. Wilhelm. He is from Los Angeles, and he should be able to help you. Are you available at nine o'clock tomorrow morning? He'll be here in this tent in cubicle number six."

Bill smiled for the first time. "That would be great."

"O.K. then. I have you down for your appointment. Wait here, and I'll get you your medicine. I'll be right back." After five minutes, she returned with the pills. "Here. The directions are on the bottle. Go to your tent, take them as prescribed, get some rest, and come back in the morning."

"Thank you so much. I hope they work."

"They will." She stood and led the grateful man to the exit.

She continued her duties.

Another knock.

"Come in," Sarah beckoned without looking up from the paperwork a medic had delivered to her.

A National Guard's man stepped into her office.

"May I help you?" Sarah said lifting her head.

"No, ma'am, but I may be able to help you."

"How so?"

"Well, Dr. Richards, I understand your cousin is missing."

Sally jumped to her feet. "Yes! Do you have any news? Have they found her?" She blurted out the words.

"We may have. When you advised the FEMA director, John Wheaton, about your cousin, Jeannine Blyer, he initiated a search. Many survivors have not been identified. There is a burned patient at the UC Davis Medical Center in Sacramento who caught our attention. Apparently, she was ejected from her vehicle during the impact. Her purse with her identification was destroyed or blown away. Although, many miles from the explosion, she received burns over 30% of her body. A chemically induced coma to help her to heal was performed. This has kept her unconscious since the event."

"Wait. Stop. Wait!" exclaimed Sally impatiently. "Why do you think she might be my cousin?"

"Because she had on her wrist a charred gold bracelet with 'Jeannie' written on one side. On the other, it read 'Love, your cousin, Sally, June 9, 2018.'"

Sally's heart felt like it would leap from her chest. "That's her birthday! I gave that bracelet to her last year! Thank you so much. You can go now. I have much to do."

The soldier smiled. "I hope she's O.K." He turned and left.

Sally barely heard him as she gathered up her things, planning as she moved. I must get to Jeannie. Things are under control, here. I'll entrust my duties to Dr. Kessler. I must call and notify Ben on the satellite phone in John Wheaton's motor home. Where's Joe? I must find transportation and leave for a few days. Can I even get to Jeannie? How did she survive? Slow down. Think. Maybe Mr. Wheaton will help me. He already has. Oh, thank God!

CHAPTER 16
Cousin Found?

Thursday, November 2, 2019 6:30 a.m. Day 6

The *whomp, whomp* sound of the helicopter blades proved deafening as Sally, skirt and hair whipping in the downdraft, climbed aboard the rear of the army chopper. Joe confirmed the dust had dissipated sufficiently, and no longer posed a threat to the turbine engines of the new C47K Chinook. Used in the last two years of the Afghanistan War to haul evacuees and supplies throughout the rough terrain, it made an ideal aircraft to haul the injured and move as many as fifty-five troops or 28,000 lbs. of relief cargo for one voyage.

The aircraft slowly lifted off the tarmac and headed northeast. As dawn broke, she stared out the window trying to make out the crater produced by the meteorite, but they were too far east. Poor visibility prevented her from seeing beyond a few miles.

John Wheaton made all the arrangements. Ben had been called and was on his way to meet Sally at the Sacramento International Airport. They planned to go together to the medical center to see Jeannie and positively identify her.

Sally glanced down at the watch Steve Harding gave her three years ago for her thirtieth birthday. She wore the watch most of the time, hurting less and less as the memory of their relationship faded. Thirty-five minutes had passed.

Outside the window, the vineyards gave way to houses forming community developments indicating they were flying over a suburb. Joined buildings formed a mall with a parking lot, empty at this early hour. We must be on the outskirts of Sacramento, thought Sally. We'll be landing soon. A recruit walked through the fuselage checking seatbelts. She glanced around at the other passengers. Three quarters of the forty-something people on board wore military uniforms. The rest were probably like her, getting special permission to be aboard for who knew what reasons.

This time, deplaning, the rotors were shut down as two National Guards' men gave her a hand. She looked around and saw a middle-aged man waving. She pointed to her chest and he nodded.

"You're Doctor Sally Richards, right? Here. Let me get that for you," extending his hand to lift her carry-on suitcase into the waiting van. "I'm Todd. I will drive you to the main terminal to meet your relative."

Sally nodded. "Mr. Wheaton thought of everything, didn't he? I thought I would have to get a taxi. Thanks."

"I will drop you off at the US Airways terminal to meet your cousin-in-law. His flight arrives in twenty minutes, so the timing is good. He knows you're coming since he was informed by Mr. Wheaton's personnel of the arrangements." He handed her a business card and cell phone. "Call me when you've picked up Ben in baggage claim. I'll be parked in the cell phone lot."

They exited the secure area, and navigated their way around the airport to the main terminal and pulled up to "arrivals".

Fifteen minutes went by when a group of passengers arriving, rode down the escalator to the baggage claim area. They saw each other at the same time. Sally began waving frantically. Tears streamed down her face when he grabbed her and gave her his customary bear hug.

"It's so good to see you!" Sally chimed in his ear. "Let's get your bag. We have a ride to the medical center. Oh, it's so good to see you." She gave him a final squeeze and let go.

"Sally, I can't tell you how excited I am to be here! I know it's going to be rough, with what you told me about Jeannie's condition. And by the way, I know it's her and she is alive. It has to be."

"Ben, I'm also sure. What color is your bag? The suitcases are coming."

"There it is." He retrieved it from the moving belt, and they headed for the door as Sally dialed the number given to her by Todd, their escort.

In the vehicle, she silently prayed they were right.

CHAPTER 17
A New World Direction

Thursday, November 2, 2019 6:45 a.m. Day 6

"Good morning, Mr. President," announced the President's Chief of Staff.

The treadmill slowed from a high-pitched whine to a steady hum as the fit, middle-aged, President Vail slackened his pace from a run to a steady cool-down walk.

"Come in. Come in," the leader of the free world beckoned. I'm almost finished. I received your memo late last night John, and I agree. We need to have a summit with all key leaders of the world as soon as it can be arranged. I'm glad you are already on that. You're a good man."

John walked closer to his boss and continued, "I've been up most of the night, sir, making phone calls around the world. Most everyone is on board with our plans. I have a

few *Quest*ions to ask you before our national security briefing begins at 9:30 a.m.

The machine ground to a halt. An aide approached the
President and handed him a towel. Taking it and wiping his
face, he turned his full attention to his scheduler and top advisor, John Peale. "Go ahead. We can sit over there on those
chairs by the window. George, if you'll excuse us?" The aide
quickly left the president's private workout room.

John drove right to the point. "We have never had such
bi-partisan support in all the thirty-odd years I have been in
this town. We need to act while everyone is willing. The top
governments are in agreement for the first time I can remember. I propose we take a vote this morning and run with
it. We need to propose to Congress a bill to appropriate the
necessary funds along with the authority to proceed with the
Space Program, immediately. Our national security depends
on it. Have you read your President's Daily Brief this morning?"

"Yes, I did. I must say it is disconcerting. Should I
make the announcement to them, today? Or do you recom-
mend we wait?

"No. I say we tell the appropriate leaders, including the
Security Council, today. But I wanted to run a few things by
you before the daily briefing. I have additions to the pro-
posed plans of action etched out. I'll show you the high-
lights, if you want, before the meeting."

"All right. I'd better get back downstairs. Have you eat-
en breakfast?"

"No. That would be great."

"Well, come on. Louise fixes the best eggs Benedict in
Washington, D.C. We can talk more, then."

"Sounds good."

****

After a quick shower and breakfast, the President, John, and two secret service men entered the elevator descending them down to the ground floor, just outside the White House kitchen. They passed a short, vaulted hallway and through a greenhouse-like antechamber called the Palm Room. Outside, they walked along the colonnade and rose garden entering the Oval Office on the southeast, sunny corner of the White House.

The President, still in awe of his personal office, scanned the famous room extending 35- feet in length with an 18-foot ceiling. He loved the history of the place. William Howard Taft, in 1909, designed it oval, giving it a homey feel. Franklin D. Roosevelt rebuilt it to this location in 1934, making it a more wheelchair friendly area, closer to the residence.

He walked over to the senior staff members, waiting, and bid them to be seated for their usual quick daily briefing.

At exactly 9:27, an aide signaled the President to disengage, so he could attend the daily intelligence briefing. National security aides in black SUVs from all around the capitol, or others on foot from other offices in the West Wing made their way to attend this meeting—among them, the director of national intelligence; the national-security adviser; and the senior adviser for counterterrorism.

After an aide announced the President of the United States, Sebastian Vail formally entered the room and sat down at the twenty-eight-foot table. At this cue, the members joined him in their seats.

"Let's get to work ladies and gentlemen," began the leader. "I have a major discovery to reveal. The most highly respected and reliable scientists in the world have concurred. It will be the thrust of our discussions today."

He cleared his throat and revealed, "More debris from the asteroid, Seriod, could impact Earth in 2058."

Several mouths fell open.

He continued. "Our planet is on an orbital collision course with at least three more remnants of the celestial body that broke apart after colliding with another asteroid two years ago. One is a half-mile in diameter and would end life on Earth as we know it. We have until then to alter our future." His glance moved from person to person to judge their reaction. They had discussed many threats before—global strikes by terrorists, unrest in various parts of the world, and global warming.

Still, their eyes widened in fear.

He added, "We could go extinct like the dinosaurs."

"Who all knows about this?" asked the national-security advisor, Bob Nelson, breaking the silence that choked the room.

The President turned his head toward the end of the table. "After the meteorite pummeled San Francisco, we immediately ordered a few universities with access to observatories and recorded data, to expedite everything they had compiled, to our NASA scientists, concerning an additional threat of another impact. Although there appeared nothing would hit the Earth in the next few years, in 2058 we will have a 99% chance of an impact. So, these scientists, all sworn to silence, key world government leaders, and we, are the only ones who know about the pending danger."

The director of national intelligence interjected, "We need to have a global Summit, while we have their support, and decide our plan of action. It needs to be arranged as soon as possible."

The President nodded. "I agree. We're already on it. Three areas must be addressed. They will take top priority at the Summit. First, we need to destroy or divert the incoming celestial objects. Second, if an impact is unavoidable, we will prepare for as many key people to survive on Earth as possible. And third, a select few people will leave our planet to settle, somewhere to be decided, in our solar system. In other words, we need to scramble the Space Program. I believe this is possible. There is no room for political squabbling or a tight budget. It will have to be a bi-partisan venture if our species is to survive."

His top security advisors nodded in agreement.

Except one.

The director of national intelligence, who asked, "How do we know this is going to work?"

The President stared at the skeptical man. "It has to."

****

"Lower your head, sir."

President Vail ducked while entering "Cadillac One," the commander-in-chief's limousine, and sat down on the rear, plush leather seat. Across from him sat Senator Paul Stevens, Republican from Illinois, and the President's personal secretary, Suzanne, a petite middle-aged lady who had worked for the President for years before he lived on Pennsylvania Avenue.

"We have a few minutes to get a bite to eat. How about Burt's Chili? It's the best in town. We'll send Stewart and Louis in to get some, and we can eat it while we ride."

"That sounds good for a November day," replied the white-haired senator.

"Great. I'll have them call ahead."

The President smiled at his passengers. He trusted Paul, and he was a hard worker.

It felt refreshing to get out of the "Big White Barn," as he lovingly called the White House. The impromptu lunch excursion gave him a chance to relax and think. He closed his eyes. I need to talk to the senator, since he specializes in foreign affairs. The appropriate country leaders to attend my summit is crucial. His eyes opened and he gazed out the window and pondered. I need England, France, China and Russia, of course, being the permanent members of the Security Council. But I'd also like Germany's Chancellor to attend. Canada and Japan need to be there because they're partners in our space program. My Chief of Staff has been putting in a lot of hours on this summit. He needs to be rewarded when this is all over.

"Mr. President?"

Drawn away from his inner space, he turned to Suzanne. He studied her for a moment. She always reminded him of a librarian with her chestnut hair braided on top of her head.

"Yes?" He smiled at her. She was the best secretary he ever had — loyal, efficient and knowledgeable.

"Sir, the plan to invite members of the rescue and recovery team in California, along with the other recipients, to the White House is complete. The date has been set for January 13th. The Summit will be over, and the space expansion program approved. I have checked your calendar, and it fits nicely with the anticipated plans for the letters to be given to Sally Richards and Joe Cooper as you requested. We could do the ceremony and give them the letters at the same time. What do you think?"

"That's a great idea, Suzanne. Get on that."

He faced his friend, the senator. Paul's head almost touched the roof of the automobile, making the President feel shorter than his six-foot frame.

"Paul, my staff is planning the Summit to take place from December 4th through the 8th. We don't have much time to prepare, but with your expertise in these affairs, you could help with the arrangements and protocol. How about it? You might get to meet a couple of leaders." He winked and raised his eyebrows.

"I'd be honored, Mr. President. Have your staff send me the details of who will be here and where, and I'll head it up."

"We have secured the Bunn Intercultural Center Auditorium at Georgetown University for the Summit meetings. We will have a formal dinner, on Wednesday night. Wives and husbands are invited. It will be held at the "big white barn." Suzanne will give you more details when we have them."

Senator Stevens laughed. "I don't know how you came up with that name, 'big white barn.' But it sure is funny."

"My daughter. When we first moved into the White House, Tessie said it looked like a big white barn. The name stuck."

The limousine, with flags waving, slowed down and pulled over to the side of a narrow street.

"We're here. We can only come when it's unexpected. The road is too narrow to suit the secret service. But they know I love the chili. You will too."

The phone rang.

As the President answered the call, three secret service men exited the Suburban behind the President's vehicle and stepped quickly into a small restaurant. People on the sidewalk waved with wide-open eyes of amazement, jumping up and down while stern men stood by the limo with eyes scanning the newly forming crowd. The President's black car was unmistakable with the waving flags on the hood, and the three other cars in the motorcade. After two minutes, the president's men in the restaurant returned, and the leader of the United States rolled down the window to receive the brown bag. He smiled his famous smile and waved to the people.

The total scene took three minutes and twenty seconds.

The line of vehicles pulled away from the curb, police escort lights flashing, while the President opened the bag and distributed Burt's famous chili to his two other passengers. He swung a small table into position between them, and said, "You can set your containers on the table. They won't spill. It's covered with a slip free material. Put some cheese on top before it gets cold." The smell of the chili permeated the Cadillac. "Don't worry about the rest of the entourage. They'll all eat later. Dig in."

The three conversed and ate, and in ten minutes, they turned into the driveway of the "big white barn."

"Just leave everything, the guys will clean up." A secret service man opened the President's door and he stepped out onto the back portico.

The rest of the afternoon the Commander in Chief attended briefings covering everything from intelligence to the economy, federal activity, and foreign policy including more meetings on the upcoming Summit.

At 6:30 p.m., President Vail adjourned to his living quarters for dinner with his wife and two children after which he helped Sebastian, his eight-year-old, with his homework. Two hours later, he continued working, answering e-mails and phone calls until after midnight. At 1:00 a.m., he lay in bed staring at the ceiling, and wondered if he would convince the world and his fellow leaders to support him in his strategy to prepare for the pending disaster in 2058.

CHAPTER 18
Joe Visits the Crater

Thursday, November 9, 2019 11:20 a.m., Day 13

"Come on in, Joe. It's open." John Wheaton, dressed in sweats, held the door ajar as Joe climbed up the steps of the FEMA director's motorhome one more time, remembering to wipe his feet on the coarse sisal mat set out by Susie. "Glad you finally remembered to do that. Have you eaten?" he asked Joe, grinning. The scientist nodded. "Honey, would you get Joe and me some coffee?"

Joe moved over to the camper table where they had their daily briefings and sat down.

"John, I'm glad to see you are working out. Listen, I have great news. I finished my rounds and the readings all concur. The levels of pollutants in the air have shrunk to within ten percent of normal. We don't need to wear our Robux masks anymore, and aircraft are safe to fly into the Impact Event area. I would like to take readings over the crater and conduct more tests to be sure, but I believe it's within limits."

John put a towel around his neck and sat down across from Joe displaying a wide grin. "At last! I'll order a chopper, immediately. I've been dying to take a first-hand look at the new landscape around ground zero. We'll go tomorrow."

Susie handed Joe coffee. "Milk and four Splenda. Just the way you like it." Joe smiled up at John's wife.

"Thank you, Mrs. Wheaton." He liked the pretty middle-aged woman. She reminded him of his mother. She seemed to take a shine to him, spoiling him with invitations to supper, most nights. They talked often about the meteor impact, and how it had changed their outlook on life. Thankfully, neither one had lost any family members. Joe frequently noticed her walking to the "Big Top" where she visited the injured and talked to the soldiers, helping when she could.

He turned back to the FEMA director. "Tomorrow would be great. I'll get everything ready that I need. Who all will be going?"

"Just a few of us for the first trip. You and I and two other scientists. That's it. Right now, the area is a Prohibited Fly Area. When you give the O.K. that it's safe, we'll start allowing other aircraft around the crater zone. There will be protocol to go by, determining who will be given access. The news media have hounded us. We'd be bombarded with news helicopters if we gave all of them clearance. The President has a plan worked out. We've been scanning the area by satellite, taking pictures and measurements. The crater is filled with seawater creating a new bay and coastline. The surface temperatures have cooled around the perimeter and we may be able to land somewhere on the newly formed coastline. I have a map we'll go over this afternoon. You'll need to let me know where you and the other two scientists want to go. They will also take tests and collect samples. Do you have any other *Quest*ions?"

"No. That about covers it. What time do you want to get together this afternoon?"

"Three-thirty. I have meetings until then."

Joe drank his last sip of coffee and stood. "O.K., John, if that's it I'll go write out my reports." He turned to Susie. "Thanks for the coffee."

She smiled. "See you later."

At nine a.m. the fog cleared. Joe rechecked his instruments, one last time, when a corporal approached.

"Are you ready to load that box onto the chopper?" the National Guardsmen asked.

"Sure. But please be careful. It's fragile." Joe didn't take his eyes off the soldier until the precious container rested on the helicopter. In his hand Joe held a portable air quality device. He would utilize it during the flight.

Hearing steps behind him, the scientist turned to see a dark figure walking briskly across the field toward him. Cupping his hand over his brow to shield his eyes from the bright morning sun, John Wheaton appeared smiling.

"Good morning!" the director shouted. "It sure is good not to need that filter mask." He inhaled a deep breath. "You're early," he added. "That's good. The pilots of the 'Little Bird' are saying the fog has burned off to the North. As soon as the others get here, we'll get going."

The two scientists arrived and surrendered their equipment to be packed on board beside Joe's container. At 9:30, they shook hands and climbed into the MH-6, nicknamed Little Bird. The rotary blades began turning as the whine of the turbine engine spooled.

The aircraft lifted off and turned right to a northerly heading. Joe scanned the distant horizon, and determined the visibility to be about ten miles. A perfect day for November. Fifty-four degrees. He turned on his air quality indicator and adjusted the settings. In the normal range.

Gaining altitude, the co-pilot turned and shouted over the single turbine engine's whine, "We'll be flying at 4,500 feet mean sea level, until we get closer to the Impact Event area. When we get to the rim, we'll descend, and you can advise us which way you want to go. We'll be there in about ten minutes."

John Wheaton shouted back, "Let's circle the newly formed bay area, and find a place to land if possible."

Joe gazed out the window at the barren terrain below. The landscape reminded him of the desert, with occasional remnants of human construction rising out of the dust. Vegetation was nonexistent. Water filled valleys in many places, creating islands and lakes. A smell of sulphur entered his nostrils getting stronger as the chopper flew closer and closer to ground zero. Newly formed inlets appeared, growing wider as the aircraft traveled north. Joe's stomach lurched as he thought he saw the edge of the rim become visible.

"Is that the rim?" he blurted.

The pilot nodded.

"We've reached the city limits of what used to be the city of San Francisco."

Joe's eyes lowered to gaze below. Water. This is the burial ground for over two million people who were vaporized in their sleep. He felt sickened and choked back tears.

No one spoke until the pilot asked, "Which way do you want to go, east or west?" The curved rim formed islands that stood out in the distance. Joe estimated they rose two hundred feet above the water. Breaks in the shoreline allowed the sea to flow into the newly formed circular crater. Topographical measurements from satellites estimated the

Impact Event Area extended miles wide, and hundreds of feet deep.

"East," replied the scientist, named Paul Carr. "The rim should be the most stable there, and we might find a place to land. I would like to gather a few rocks to take back to my laboratory."

Joe studied Paul. He seemed like a nice guy, arriving from Harvard yesterday. Last night, at the Marriott, Paul walked up to him and introduced himself. While eating together, Joe learned the renowned head of the Department of Earth and Planetary Studies had written several books, and researched meteor impacts and their effects on mankind.

Next to Paul, another scientist named Charles Lamont sat tapping a computer connected to a portable Geiger counter.

John Wheaton stared out the window and back to the map on his lap.

Frustration in his voice, he said, "I can't make anything out of this map. I hope you pilots know where you are going."

The pilot in the left front seat smiled back at him and said, "Don't worry, sir, we have a satellite-generated map that is accurate, and GPS readings. We're over the Oakland area, and we've descended to 1,000 feet above ground level. If the scientists think it's safe, we'll find a place to land." Everyone except Joe nodded.

Hovering above the rim, Joe estimated the mound extended approximately forty-feet-wide. It plunged steeply down to the water on one side. The surface had ridges and crevices with shiny rock formations strewn everywhere.

Not much of a place to land, thought Joe.

"Hey, guys. Do you think it's safe to put this thing down?" Joe offered.

"We need to get samples of rock and displaced soil," said Paul. "I'm sure we can find an open place up ahead."

The pilots shrugged as they eyed each other and returned to their search for a clear sight to land the helicopter.

Five minutes passed and the co-pilot said, "Over there." The craft banked to the right and circled to land into the wind. Dust blew everywhere as they approached the surface.

Safely on the ground, Joe monitored his portable air quality device and affirmed the atmosphere was within tolerable limits.

The rotor blades stopped, and everyone except the pilots stepped down to the ground one by one.

"This is eerie and exciting at the same time, isn't it?" John Wheaton remarked. "I'm going to take pictures." He walked off.

Joe wrinkled his nose as he scanned the area. The smell of sulphur, smelling like rotten eggs, filled his nostrils. The brownish-red terrain reminded him of the pictures of Mars he'd seen on the computer. He bent over and touched the ground. Still warm. A shiny, green stone, smooth like glass, caught his eye. He rolled it over in his hand. Tektite, formed by the heat and pressure of the impact.

Charles walked along the rim studying the ground. He bent over and picked up samples of rock and debris and put them in a bag he carried.

Paul pulled his box of instruments out of the helicopter and began assembling them on the barren surface.

Joe lifted his own container of instruments and set them on the ground. As he set up the dust monitor, he heard a shriek come from the other side of the aircraft. Stunned, he bolted around the chopper as he heard a descending yell that grew faint as he ran toward it.

Paul came running and almost tripped over a stone as he approached.

"Who was that?" the alarmed man from Harvard shouted to Joe.

"I don't know. But someone's in trouble," Joe said as he scanned the area. Off in the distance, he made out the FEMA director who appeared to be taking pictures in his bright orange parka.

"Where is Charles?"

"That's a good question," Joe said.

"Wait! Listen." Splashing could barely be heard from over the edge of the crater. Paul and Joe ran to where the rim dropped down to the bay. There, floundering, gasped Charles.

"Help!" he shouted, mouth filling with water. "I can't climb out. The bank is too steep and the stones are loose. Help me!"

Joe turned toward the parked helicopter. The pilots napped in the cockpit.

"Hey!" He shouted, waving his arms and running toward them.

When he stopped at the aircraft he opened the door and yelled, "Wake up! We need help. One of the scientists fell down the bank and into the water. Do you have any rope, or a life preserver?"

The lieutenant jumped out of the front seat and yanked the cushion off the chair behind him. "Throw this to him. It's a floatation device."

"Thanks." Joe grabbed the cushion and ran back to the edge of the rim by Paul. With a big heave, he tossed the cushion like a shot putter, as far as he could down the bank. The cushion almost hit Charles on the head.

Charles seized it and held on tight. "This water is freezing! Get me out of here," he shouted. "I can't stand this much longer."

"We'll try to get the helicopter to help you. Hold on!"

Running back to the helicopter, the pilot yelled, "Get in!"

He jumped in the aircraft as the rotor blades began to turn. About a hundred yards down the rim, Joe saw John Wheaton running toward them from a distance waving his arms.

The aircraft lifted off its landing sight and slowly rose up into the sky.

The pilot yelled to Joe, "We'll have to be careful that the rotor blades don't hit the bank. This is going to be very tricky. I'm going to maneuver the chopper down so Mr. Lamont can grab the landing skid, which are the rails the helicopter rests on when on the ground. Hopefully, he'll understand and hang on. We'll try to get him to swim away from the steep bank. I don't know what else we can do before he's too cold to latch on."

Joe's stomach churned. He knew the water had to be about sixty degrees in this part of California, during November.

The pilot lowered "Little Bird" down close to the water.

Please grab the skid, prayed Joe.

"I can't get any lower or closer to the shore line," shouted the pilot.

Joe watched Charles struggle below. The man slowly paddled toward the helicopter, with one hand swimming and the other arm clutched around the seat cushion.

The water swirled and churned as the craft hovered.

At last, the wet, drowning scientist reached for the skid and grabbed it. The life preserver bobbed and floated away. Joe gave a thumbs up indication to the pilot, and with great care, lifted the man out of the water.

Please hold on, thought Joe.

Raising up over the rim, Charles clung to the skid. As the helicopter hovered, Paul and John Wheaton grabbed the frightened scientist and pulled him out of the way of the aircraft so it could land. The man fell to the ground, exhausted.

When the rotors stopped, the pilots jumped out, and retrieved a blanket they kept behind the seats in case of emergencies.

Joe took it and ran over to Charles.

"Here, this will help," he said, draping the wool covering over the shivering man. "That was a close one! Are you all right? What happened?"

"Thank you for the blanket," the wet man said, shuddering. "My arms are sore, and I have a few bruises, but I think I'm O.K. I was walking too close to the edge. I didn't realize it, but all of a sudden my feet slipped and the stones gave way. I slid all the way down to the water before I stopped. I don't know how I survived. I don't swim very well."

Joe pointed at the pilots. "You can thank them. They sure know how to fly that thing."

The pilot smiled. "I had a tour in Afghanistan in search and rescue. We had to fly into some close quarters in the villages. At least, this time, we didn't have anyone shooting at us."

John interjected, "Let's get this man back to Woodside. They can check him over, carefully, there."

They quickly gathered their gear and boarded the helicopter.

The "Big Top" stood out above the wasted terrain as the helicopter approached Woodside from the north. Joe watched the tent grow larger as the pilots pointed it out to their passengers. The aircraft circled, made its approach to the makeshift helipad and touched down. Waiting until the rotors stopped, medics carrying a stretcher, ran and opened the door.

John Wheaton smiled at them and commented, "Glad to see you guys received my satellite text. This man is freezing, and has many bruises. You need to warm him up and check him over. He took a dip in the crater."

The medics asked Charles to lie down onto the lowered stretcher. They covered him with blankets and carried him toward the big tent.

After they disappeared into the opening, John Wheaton turned to Joe and said, "I want to see you in my camper as soon as you put your instruments away."

Joe nodded, and the group went their separate ways. He thought he knew why the FEMA director wanted to talk to him—his job here was finished. The Robux Filter enabled thousands to be rescued, and now he could go home. What home? He had no home.

He would get a divorce and begin a new life.

CHAPTER 19
Dan's Interview

Tuesday, November 21, 2019, 8:00 a.m. Day 25

Reporter: *"Good evening. Welcome to the Ted James Show, here on WCTE world-wide television network. Tonight, we have with us, Dan Alexander. Thank you for being with us, tonight, Mr. Alexander."*

Dan: *"It's my pleasure."*

Reporter: *"So, tell us. Rumors are flying. Are you and Kristen officially engaged?"*

Dan: *"Yes, we are engaged. No date for the wedding has been set, but we're thinking we'll say our vows sometime in the summer. The family is very excited.*

Reporter: *"How is your leg feeling these days? When will you get your prosthesis?"*

Dan: *"It is healing pretty fast, actually. I think I'll be fitted for a bionic prosthesis in two months. The artificial leg should be indiscernible from a real one, once I get used to it. Doctors say someday we'll be all spare parts. I can't wait."*

Reporter: *"Do you have any residual pain?"*

Dan: *"Actually, I have a lot of discomfort, but I'm diligently working in physical therapy every day. The hurting is what they call phantom pain. I can still feel sensations in my missing limb. Eventually, it should go away."*

Reporter: *"Are you planning to run for office in the future, like members of your family? Especially, since you've earned your law degree."*

Dan: *"If the country wants and needs me, I will run."*

Reporter: *"When?"*

Dan: *"Whenever the people want me."*

Reporter: *"How does Kristen feel about that?"*

Dan: *"As you know, she has politicians in her family, like I do. She will support me in any endeavors I might have."*

Reporter: *"Is it true, you have been invited to the White House in a few days?"*

Dan: *"It's true. January 13th. Kristen will be there, too. I believe you'll be televising it."*

Reporter: *"Yes, we will. Well, our time is almost up. Do you want to add anything before wrapping things up?"*

Dan: *"Yes, Ted, I'd like to thank everyone in the world who sent me get well wishes, and letters of encouragement during my time of physical hardship. It has meant a great deal to me, Kristen, and our families. And I will be eternally grateful."*

Reporter: *"Thank you, Dan. We wish you and Kristen best wishes, and for you a speedy recovery. We'll be anticipating your endeavors in the future. Coming up next, Justin Bieber. Stay tuned."*

CHAPTER 20
Jeannie's Phone Call

"Jeannie! Is that you? I'm so glad you are finally able to talk on the phone. How are you feeling today? Did your grafting go well?"

"Yes, Sally. The doctors say it went well. It'll be a while before I'll be able to move my shoulder where they operated. I have a cast. But the procedure was a success. My jaw is still sore. Ben says hello."

"Tell him I said, hi. I've been talking to him every day since I've been back in New York. Is he taking good care of you? I can't believe it's been a month since we found you. Ben told me you are able to talk now, since the bandages have been removed from your mouth area."

"Ben hasn't left my side except to eat since you and he found me here in Sacramento. As he probably told you, I've been awake three weeks, but I couldn't move my jaw. They removed the bandages from around my mouth and jaw when they grafted skin to my shoulder. I don't look so good, Sally. The pain isn't as bad as it was, though."

"You'll always be beautiful to the ones who love you and your hair will grow back. I'm glad they are keeping the pain under control. You are lucky to have survived."

"You're right. Burns over thirty percent of my body was pretty bad. But I'm healing."

"Have they said when you can be moved back to Colorado?"

"They're saying I could get a mission plane, provided by contributors and volunteers, to fly us back to Denver next week, but it'll depend how my shoulder does."

"That would be great, Jeannie."

"Sally, I had to call to wish you a happy birthday. I didn't forget your special day is tomorrow. How are you doing, anyway? You're back to work, aren't you? Have you heard from the ones you worked with in California? Ben's been telling me about them. He said you even met the President."

Sally smiled. "Thank you for remembering my birthday. I can't believe I will be thirty-four years old, tomorrow. Yes, I did meet the President. And guess what? I have been invited to the White House in a month from now on January 13th. Can you believe it?"

"Wow! That's great."

"I've been keeping in touch with a scientist named Joe, who I worked with at Woodside Triage. I wish he didn't live so far away. He's pretty good looking and about my age. We talk every week. He calls me on Saturdays."

"Whoa. Sounds like possibilities, Sally. Have you heard from Steve?"

"No. We're done, Jeannie. I'm sure he's deep into his training in Houston."

"Ben told me you met Dan Alexander. Is he as handsome in person as he is in the magazines? He had an interview on television a little over a week ago. Did you see it?"

"Yes, I did," replied Sally, "And yes, he's more handsome in person. He's engaged."

"Oh, I know," Jeannie answered. "I have been hearing rumors that he may run for Congress next election. Is that true?"

"Probably. Because I've heard the same rumors."

Jeannie continued, "What do you think of the Summit this week? It finishes up today. Did you hear they are going to accelerate the Space Program?"

"Yes. They're trying to get my hopes up." Sally rolled her eyes.

"You haven't given up on NASA?"

"No, I haven't."

"Good for you. Well, Sally, I'm getting a little tired and my jaw is hurting. My face isn't completely healed, yet."

"O.K., Jeannie. You managed quite well. It was sure great to hear your voice. You were unconscious when I saw you in the Burn Center. Please call me often. I love you."

"I love you, too. Good bye, Sally."

She tossed her cell phone onto the bed and gazed at the Hudson River.

I have nothing to wear. I've been invited to the White House, and I have nothing appropriate to wear!

CHAPTER 21
The Summit

Monday, December 4, 2019, 7:30 a.m., Day 38

"Is the translation equipment ready, Paul?"

"Yes, Mr. President. The interpretation system is up and functional. There are twelve channels, so you should understand every word. The switches are labeled with who's speaking. Everyone will have a set."

The first lady straightened her husband's tie. "There you go, sweetheart, now it's straight."

"I believe that completes our briefing. Do you have all my notes and my speech?"

"Yes, sir, everything is in your briefcase. David is carrying it, and he'll be right behind you as you enter the auditorium."

At the cue of the senator, the President and his entourage moved out into the hall and descended down the stairs to the south portico. The six-vehicle procession rolled out of the long driveway, circled the White House to Pennsylvania

Avenue, and turned left toward Georgetown. Inside Cadillac One the President practiced his speech and went over protocol with Senator Paul Stevens.

Minutes later, he raised his head and spoke. "Did everyone show up? I received a report Hu Jintao's airplane had weather delays."

"Yes. Everyone made it," Paul assured him. "And everything is ready."

The black limousine pulled up to the Bunn Intercultural Center in the heart of Georgetown University. Rows of policemen lined the walkway to the entrance. Crowds waited behind ropes waiting to get a glimpse of the world leaders who would begin filing into the Center at 9:00 a.m. The media stood poised with cameras and recorders, their mobile vans, with antennas up, parked nearby. Paul initiated instructions for the arrivals to be spaced about two minutes apart to avoid congestion and ensure security measures.

President Vail anticipated greeting the heads of state and governments inside the building.

Right on schedule, the rulers of much of the world, surrounded by a throng of security personnel, exited their limos and marched to the entrance, one by one.

"It's my pleasure to see you, again," the President said to each leader when he entered. They shook hands and smiled. Cameras flashed.

Escorted into the auditorium, where the media was prohibited, the rulers moved to assigned seats. The President stepped on to the stage, smiling. The room became silent as he stood at the podium to present his introductory oration:

"Your Excellencies, Distinguished delegates, Observers and guests, Ladies and Gentlemen,

It is with the utmost gratitude and urgency, that I extend my appreciation for your presence at this Summit. We gather in response to the catastrophe of October 28, 2019, and the pending demise of the human race by a greater Impact Event in the year 2058. As you have been informed, this collision will be the result of the Earth's orbit crossing the path of the remnants of the asteroid, Seriod. I implore you, to work together, to discuss and produce a plan, through joint effort, to prevent this destruction from happening.

This pending collision will be comparable to the meteor that destroyed the dinosaurs. Life as we know it will cease to exist. Ninety percent of all life forms on our planet will die. The Earth will be changed for millenniums.

We all have a new common enemy. Its name is time.

We must work together this week to set goals to minimize or prevent this from happening. Our Earth is vulnerable and fragile. Being life forms with superior intelligence and development, it is our responsibility to preserve ourselves, so we can continue to be a species in our universe. We owe this to posterity.

I have a number of proposals.

First, and utmost, we need to tap the brains of our experts to arrest this collision from happening in the first place.

If this fails, we need to ensure the survival of as many people as possible. We could create biospheres over population clusters for as many life forms as we are able to save—a Noah's Ark, so to speak.

Another means of accomplishing this goal is to proliferate the Space Program using worldwide means and cooperation. The United States proposes a new international endeavor called the Great Hope Project. Our ambition is to put permanent colonies into outer space starting with the moon, Mars, and free space structures, similar to the International

Space Station. We have visions of increasing the number of colonies, eventually, to thirteen.

There are many possibilities.

In conclusion, I am optimistic of the outcome of this Summit. I know we can work together for the common good of humanity. I look forward to fruitful discussions and a permanent solution to this crisis."

The President of the United States of America stepped down from the stage amidst a standing ovation.

Each representative had the opportunity to render a prepared response.

The Summit had begun.

****

During the next five days, the nations' leaders pounded out proposals, offering technical innovations and suggestions, previously top secret, in their respective countries. President Vail, was overwhelmed by the cooperation and willingness to attack this world wide dilemma. Commitment flourished, and funds were pledged.

At the end of the Summit, President Vail cemented all his proposals and some were added. One prospectus included a new world order, by expanding the powers of the United Nations. This would be a debate for the future.

The Commander in Chief adjourned the Summit on Friday.

In the limo traveling back to the White House, the President smiled at Paul Stevens. "That could not have gone better. I want to express my deep appreciation for a job well accomplished. I could not have done it without you. When do you travel to Illinois?"

"This afternoon, sir. And thank you. You did a splendid job yourself."

President Vail closed his eyes. Step one is completed. Now I need a report on how Project Great Hope at the Johnson Space Center is progressing.

CHAPTER 22
Anticipation

Saturday, January 13, 2020 4:00 p.m. Day 78

Sally stood peering out the lobby window of the Willard Hotel. She fidgeted as she anticipated the arrival of an official black van that would escort her and fourteen fellow invitees to a White House reception and ceremony, to be held in their honor for participating in the rescue operations after the impact of the meteorite. She still couldn't believe she, along with the others, were being awarded the Presidential Medal of Freedom.

Snowflakes fell on this thirty-degree day in January, swirling as they were caught in the draft of vehicles rushing down Pennsylvania Avenue. Several black cars sped by, but none turned into the driveway of the hotel.

A tap on the shoulder made her jump. She turned around to see a familiar face smiling at her.

"Joe!" She reached up and flung her arms around his neck giving him a hug, which he returned by wrapping his arms around her and swinging her in a circle.

"I can't believe it's been over a month since I last saw you. Look at you. You're in a dress with makeup and jewelry. It's hard to recognize you without your khaki pants and muddy shoes. You sure clean up well. You're gorgeous!"

"Oh come on, Joe, you're flattering me. Surely women wear dresses in L.A."

"Sure. But not many of them look like you. Thanks, by the way, for all the e-mails, text messages and calls. Can you believe we are going to the White House to get the Presidential Medal of Freedom and meet the President, again?"

Sally realized she had missed Joe and her stomach twinged. Butterflies? He stands a head taller than I, and my height exceeds five-foot nine inches. I love his smile. We have a lot in common. His e-mails and phone calls have revealed our similarities in views about politics, religion and NASA. And he has a great sense of humor.

"I know. It's unbelievable. And the government paid for our trips to Washington. The Willard is a five-star hotel. We could walk to the White House. It's a block down the street."

Sally scanned the massive lobby. The high, arched windows and marble pillars reminded her of a palace. Marble floors and luxurious rugs with scattered sitting areas dotted the room. A porter pushed a cart, creaking as it moved, loaded with bags toward the elevator, disturbing the music of Mozart playing in the background. A few people gathered near the main doors. She didn't recognize anyone, until she heard another familiar voice behind her.

"There you two are. Is the van here, yet?" John Wheaton greeted them with hearty handshakes, bending forward to give her a peck on the cheek. "It's great to see you two, again, and for such an occasion. What an honor. You look beautiful, Sally."

"Thank you, Mr. Wheaton. It's great to see you, too."

Joe glanced at his watch. 4:15 p.m. "It should be here soon. Are those people going with us?" He nodded toward a gathering of about ten people clustered near the front entrance.

"Yes. I recognize most of them. They worked at other triages, in charge of various areas. Excuse me, while I go speak to them."

Joe turned back to Sally. "I heard Dan Alexander is attending the celebration with Kristen. They're engaged. Is he walking with his prosthesis, or is he in a wheelchair these days? Do you know?"

Sally raised her eyebrows and said, "I think he is still in a wheelchair, but I'm not sure.

I saw on the internet; he is staying at the Blair House. Is that true?"

Joe grinned. "Yes, it's true. And he's going to run for Congress in the next election. I think he'll be President someday."

"He'd make a good one. I read he's changed completely since the Impact. Matured. And I am for anyone who wants to expand the Space Program."

"I agree. Look. Everyone is moving toward the door. The van must be here."

Sally's heart beat faster as she as she stepped outside and sucked in a big breath of cold air. Oh my gosh. It's time to go to the "big white barn."

CHAPTER 23
At the White House

Saturday, January 13, 2020 4:30 p.m. Day 78

"Welcome to the White House, Dr. Richards. Dr. Cooper." The aide waved his hand as they stepped through the security detector into the Entrance Hall to join others who arrived before them. "I will be explaining to you the order of events, momentarily. Please wait here a few minutes while everyone assembles."

"Thank you," they answered in unison.

A female security member immediately approached them carrying a list. "Dr. Richards? Dr. Cooper? May I see your invitation and I.D.?" As they retrieved the required documents, the lady crossed off their names on her chart.

"How did you know who we were before you checked our I.D.s?" asked Sally.

"I belong to the Secret Service. We are required to memorize your pictures and names. Of course, you two were easy. You've been in all the papers and on television."

Sally tried to take it all in. A quick head count included about thirty people including reporters, wearing badges, and sporting cameras, while they sought a few words from guests. One talked to Dan Alexander and Kristen. Two more held a recorder up to John Wheaton who appeared to answer *Quest*ions. Portraits of past Presidents decorated the walls. She wiped her sweaty hands on her dress, and hoped they would be dry when it was her turn to greet people.

"This is amazing," she whispered to Joe, who also scanned the premises.

"I never in my wildest dreams ever thought I would be invited to the White House, did you?"

"Not in my wildest dreams." She gave him a big smile and a wink.

An aide held up his arm to get everyone's attention. "Ladies and gentlemen, did everyone read the protocol instructions sent to you? If not, raise your hands." Sally saw one woman lift up her hand. "Here you go." The aide handed the lady a paper. "Please read this before we go to the receiving line." He turned back to the rest of the group. "Are there any *Quest*ions?" No one responded. "If not, we will proceed to the Red Room to assemble everyone in the order in which you will be presented to the dignitaries and the President. Step this way."

They passed between the pillars into Cross Hall with marble walls and floors. Passing undercut glass chandeliers, they made their way to the Red Room. As Sally entered, she noticed why it was called the Red Room. Red twill with a gold scroll design covered the walls. The furniture, covered in silk, had the same shade of red. Here, they were given name tags and engraved cards with numbers and their names on them.

When the time came, one by one their numbers were called and they moved to the adjoining State Dining Room where six round tables filled the middle of the room, and a podium with microphones stood in front of the white fireplace. Inside the doorway, along a wall, the President waited with his Chief of Staff and other dignitaries.

At last, Sally, surrendering her card at the entrance to the famous room, heard her name being announced to the reception line. As instructed, she passed from one person to the next, shaking their hands and repeating to each one, "How do you do?"

When in front of President Vail, with bulbs flashing and a TV camera focused on her, she faced the President and said, "Nice to see you, again, Mr. President."

"Nice to see you, too, Doctor Richards."

I can't believe it. He remembered my name. The usher guided her to a seat at one of the many round tables set up in the dining area.

After three more guests were announced, she shivered when she heard Joe's name. She watched him go through the line and after he shook hands with the President the aide guided him to his seat.

"Well, this is a coincidence," Joe chuckled, as he sat down in the assigned seat next to her.

"Did you have something to do with this?"

"Maybe. But you'll never know, will you?" he remarked, grinning.

"What dish did you choose?"

"I'm having the chicken cordon bleu. How about you?"

"So am I. I guess we have the same tastes, huh? A little better than the military cuisine we ate in California."

Nerves settling down, Sally noticed the procession ended, and the President joined a table across the room and situated closest to a podium. Everyone at his table stood as he sat down. The news media snapped pictures continuously.

****

"I can't eat another bite," Sally rolled her eyes. "The food was scrumptious."

"I agree. I'm afraid if I lived here, I'd gain thirty pounds," laughed Joe.

The voice of Senator Brand announced at the podium, "Ladies and gentlemen, the President of the United States."

The Commander in Chief moved to the podium while everyone clapped.

"Thank you. Thank you. I hope you all enjoyed your dinners made by my chief chef, Louise, and her crew." Another round of applause. "Now, we'd like to present to each of you the distinguished Medal of Freedom. Once in your possession, you will be part of an elite group of recipients of the highest civilian award presented to those who have honored and served the people of America. I would personally, like to commend you on your achievements and offer my appreciation to each and every one of you who has earned this medal. You have all excelled in your own way. I am grateful. And the country is grateful. May you continue to realize your dreams, as well as prosper and contribute in future endeavors. By your example, we will always be proud of the United States of America."

One by one, each stood and made the way to the podium to receive his or her medal.

After ten people received their medals, Sally heard her name called and she rose with wobbly knees and proceeded to the podium. She thought she would faint. Standing in front of him, he hung a ribbon with the precious medal around her neck.

"Thank you, Sally Richards, for serving your country men with such skill and selfless bravery." Cameras flashed and T.V. video recorders whirred.

Sally had tears in her eyes as she shook the hand of the President once again. Everyone burst into applause. She beamed at Joe as she made her way back to their table. When seated, a White House staff member bent down to Joe and her handing them each a sealed letter.

Sally raised her eyebrows and Joe shrugged. "I don't see anyone else getting one of these, do you?" They scanned the room. The staff member vanished out the door.

"I think we are the only ones. Let's open them." The ceremony continued around them with names called and hands clapping.

The letter appeared official. Sally's eyes grew into saucers when she whispered the return address — NATIONAL AERONAUTICS AND SPACE ADMINISTRATION.

They tore open the letters together. Except for the names, they read the same. Sally's read:

Washington, D.C.
February 13, 2020

Dear Miss Richards,
    The National Aeronautics and Space Administration (NASA) is pleased to offer you a candidacy to the National Space Program. You have been selected to join the Class of March 1, 2018 at the Johnson Space Center in Houston, Texas.
    Please accept or decline this offer within ten days of the receipt of this letter.

    Upon receipt of your acceptance, additional information will be forthcoming.

    Please respond by emailing to rcmichaels@nasa.net or call 281-863-2180.

    Congratulations and we hope to meet you in March.

Regards,

Col. Ralph Michaels

Colonel Ralph Michaels
Director Johnson Space Center, Houston, Texas
National Aeronautics and Space Administration

They grabbed each other's hands and squeezed. While clapping sounded around them, Sally wanted to stand and take a bow.

She had waited over a year for this letter. It was hard to take it all in. Of course she would accept the appointment. Her mind whirled. She had a month to pack up and move to Houston. Not that far, she thought, when in three years she could be living on Mars.

CHAPTER 24
The Journey Begins

Thursday, March 1, 2020 8:00 a.m. Day 125

Sally tapped her foot and glanced at her watch once again. Candidates filed in and occupied most of the seats of Teague Auditorium at the Johnson Space Center.

"Is anyone sitting next to you?"

Sally spun her torso around toward the familiar voice. "Joe! Have a seat."

She had been searching for him for the last hour. In five minutes the doors would close and the orientation would begin with no one else allowed in the hall. She thought he hadn't made it. He had texted her, when his flight landed, to let her know that weather had delayed his flight and he would get a taxi. He must have paid the driver big bucks to get from the Houston George Bush Airport to the Johnson Space Center so fast.

Sitting next to her, his faint musk cologne permeated her nostrils, soaring her heart rate, and suddenly the room felt too warm. That cashmere sweater he has on is awesome. The green matches his eyes. I didn't know he had green eyes...

The orientation lasted four hours with a lunch break at noon. The two hundred candidates received handouts and a map labeling the one hundred buildings of the center.

Joe studied his papers. "Do you have plans for lunch? I see the astronauts' cafeteria is located around the corner in Building 3."

"I do now." She grinned and winked. They rose and walked toward the door. Sally observed the other candidates— mostly men about Joe's age of thirty something making up the majority in number. She counted no more than ten women. To qualify up to this point, all the applicants held appropriate educational backgrounds and excelled in their fields. Most had doctorates in qualifying areas such as engineering, biological science, physical science, or mathematics.

The cafeteria teemed with activity. "This is the astronauts' place to eat. Maybe we'll see someone we recognize."

Sally dreaded the thought of running into Steve Harding. She was sure he must still be training, here.

They picked up trays in line, and slid them along while choosing items of offered food.

"I'll take care of this," Joe said, pulling out his wallet at the register.

Sally tilted her head, pursed her lips, and replied, "Only if you let me buy yours next time."

"It's a deal," he answered smiling, displaying perfect white teeth.

At three o'clock, they completed their physicals and finished their scheduled first day of orientation.

"Do you want to take a walk until our bus comes and check out part of the complex?" asked Joe at their rendezvous spot in the front hall of Building 15. "I'll need to pick up my Roller board suitcase at the auditorium sometime before we catch the bus to the hotel." He studied his schedule and added, "The shuttle takes us to our hotel at four thirty. We have about an hour to walk."

"Sure, let's go."

The air felt brisk as they marched along Avenue D turning onto 5th Street at the end. Sally inhaled deeply as she walked on this March day. She glanced at Joe. Here she was at the Johnson Space Center, beginning a new adventure alongside someone who could be an important part of her future. Out of the ashes of the meteor tragedy, life appears to be renewing itself. Maybe, I'll soon find happiness.

The rest of the week consisted of endless interviews, psychological testing, and intelligence quotient evaluation. Toward the end of the grueling process, Sally noticed less and less applicants entering the shuttle bus back to the hotel. Every day she prayed it would not be her last day at the center. Thursday, the final day, she and Joe endured another more extensive physical exam in the afternoon.

At 5:00 p.m. twenty-five men and five women filed into a conference room and sat down. Colonel Ralph Michaels, former astronaut, current Director of the Johnson Space Center, and, noted Sally, the one who signed their letters of acceptance, stood in front of a mural depicting a picture of the space station that spanned the entire wall. Sitting next to Joe, she thought she would jump out of her skin any minute if the Colonel didn't speak soon.

Finally, when all became quiet, he stated, "Ladies and Gentlemen, I am proud to announce that the thirty invitees in this room will comprise the Astronaut Class of March, 2020."

Everyone, including Sally and Joe, jumped up, clapped, and yelled shouts of glee.

When they settled down, the Director continued, "Welcome to our family of past, present and future astronauts. May you experience no boundaries along the way in becoming the next generation of extra-terrestrial beings to settle on the Moon, Mars and beyond. Congratulations."

Sally closed her eyes momentarily, and thanked God for seeing her through this week. When she opened them, Joe opened his arms and threw them around her, shouting,

"We did it! We did it! Our new lives have begun."

CHAPTER 25
Would Be Astronauts

Monday, March 12, 2020, 7:00 a.m. Day 132

"Come on, Sally! You can do it! Swim, girl, swim! You have one more lap to go."

Sally's flight suit seemed to add tons to her weight and her tennis shoes felt like lead as she kicked her feet using a side stroke to complete her third and final lap in the pool. She could hear Joe encouraging her, and nearing the end, his voice gave her the needed strength until, finally, she touched the wall and raised her head and smiled at him.

"I made it," she said, half to herself. Two other candidates, waiting their turn, clapped along with Joe.

"Yes, you did," Joe answered, extending his hand and helping her out of the pool. "Here's a towel."

Sally dried herself off. "This completes the last pool test."

"Your right. For both of us," added Joe.

Ten minutes later, dressed and in her warm dry clothes, she met Joe back outside.

"Let's go get some breakfast. That ordeal was a workout. Three laps to begin with, ten minutes treading water, and then the last three laps have made me famished."

They headed toward the cafeteria. The light jacket Sally wore felt good on this warm late winter day in March. "I think it must be almost seventy degrees this morning. Maybe Spring is around the corner."

"It's nice being here in Houston." He pointed. "There are buds on that tree."

Sally raised her head and peered at the tall tree. "It's a magnolia. It can bloom as early as January, here in Houston, but most commonly about now. They bloom for two weeks and smell awesome."

"How do you know that?" he said with curiosity.

"I love trees." They climbed the steps to the cafeteria.

Joe leaned over to Sally's ear, "There's Don Pearce. He's head of the new Great Hope Project. Hopefully, he'll be our boss." He squeezed her arm.

She turned to face him. "He will, I know it."

They entered the line and picked up a tray, nodding to several people. "I can't believe how many other candidates we've met. It's feeling more like we belong here.

Sally smiled and scanned the room. Suddenly her head stopped turning and the blood drained from her face.

Joe noticed, and tried to follow her eyes. "What is it?"

Her lips dry, she managed to blurt, "He's here."

"Who's here? Is it someone I should know?" He searched the room for a famous, familiar face.

She turned to face back to the food selection, grabbing a salad and slapping it on her plate, hoping her wet hair had dried.

"Steve Harding. We were engaged a year ago. He's the guy wearing the red shirt across the room, but don't look now."

"Sally, you were engaged to an astronaut?"

She handed the checkout lady her debit card, and told her to use it for the two of them, and headed for a table in the corner. They sat down.

"Yes. But we're not now. He ditched me."

"Sally, I'm so sorry."

"Don't be. It's over." She hesitated then continued. "We went to graduate school together at Harvard, but it's been more than a year, now, and I'm over him." Their eyes locked onto each other. "I've begun a new life."

Joe's eyes brightened and his face softened, but he said nothing.

At five o'clock they entered the bus for the ride to their hotel and sat down together.

Joe spoke first. "What did you think of the altitude chamber?"

Sally, grateful to talk about something general, said, "The pressure changes bothered my ears, but I didn't have any problems. The emergency practice was comical when you couldn't concentrate at extreme pressure changes. I learned a lot."

"I did too."

She decided to change the subject. "Have you found an apartment, yet?"

"No. But we have tomorrow afternoon off. Why don't we scout the area together? Maybe we could find something close to each other. I've been searching the internet."

Uneasy, she studied him. "What are you saying?"

"We could share an apartment if you want. We could get a two-bedroom place. What do you think? I cook."

Sally's heart pounded. Was this a giant step forward? Or was he just being friendly and thinking of splitting expenses?

They spent the next afternoon reading apartment guides and driving around, south of Houston, in the car she brought from New York.

"Did you like the last one we saw, or do you like this one better?" Sally asked Joe as they walked through the Leisure Lake Apartment. "This one has three bedrooms. We could get another roommate."

Joe scowled. "That's not what I had in mind."

Sally's stomach lurched. This is getting serious. Am I ready for it? It's been almost a year since my break up with Steve Harding. Am I ready to try again? Do I really have a choice when my whole being is shouting *GO FOR IT?*

"So which one do you like, if any?" she inquired.

"I liked the first one we saw. Let's lease it."

"All right." What am I doing? My heart wins.

They drove to the Ashlar Apartments and walked into the office. The next two hours they filled out paper work and took a tour of the apartment. They would move in the following Saturday.

"Let's celebrate. I'll buy you dinner." Joe stated jovially.

Sally felt happy for the first time in a year. "Sounds great. Where do you want to eat?"

"I saw an Applebee's down the street. They have a diversified menu."

After eating, they drove to the Town Place Suites where most of the astronaut candidates stayed until they found housing.

Sally parked her car and turned to Joe, "I can't believe what I did tonight."

"What do you mean? Are you having second thoughts?"

"No. But I do need to know where I stand with you. We've been skype buddies, and email friends when you were in L.A. and I was in New York." She hesitated. "Are you indicating something else, or am I being stupid?"

He reached over and put his finger to her lips. "Shhh. You are not being stupid. I promise you, my intentions are totally honorable. But I need to tell you something I haven't told you before."

Sally's raised her eyebrows and her mouth fell open. "You're married with three kids!"

"No, I don't have three kids."

Her shoulders sank and her head leaned back on the headrest as she looked up at the ceiling. "But you're married."

"Yes."

"Why didn't you tell me?" Somewhere down deep, anger started to bubble up. *What a cad he is. What a fool I am.*

She stepped out of her Lexus, embarrassed with tears welling, slammed the door shut, ran to the entrance and bounded up the single flight of stairs to her room. She swiped the key, entered, and let the door slam behind her. Falling on the bed, she let out a groan along with a flood of tears. After the knocking on the door stopped, the phone rang several times, but she let the calls go unanswered. *I am done with men. I'll be single forever.*

****

The training continued. She enjoyed the weightless training in the KC 135 aircraft and the scuba diving, taught to simulate spacewalks. The sadness and anger lingered just below the surface of her consciousness, but, totally committed to becoming an astronaut, she ambitiously worked to be the best in the field.

Joe continued to try to entice her into a conversation, and flowers filled her new apartment, but she vowed she would not be a paramour. Finally, the calls slowed and the flowers died.

CHAPTER 26
Selected

Monday, July 2, 2020, 12:00p.m., Day 244

"Is your salad tasty?"

Shocked at the familiar voice, she raised her head to see a tall, fit, lean man with a familiar face.

"Steve!" She almost choked.

"Congratulations on making the team. I knew you would. May I sit down?"

"O.K. And thank you. It only took the President's intervention." I knew this moment had to come, sometime. I might as well get it over with.

"You deserve it. I read your name on some medical records, and I've tried to call you, but you don't answer. Are you all right?"

Face to face, she observed the bright, blue eyes that used to make her swoon. He's more toned, as if that is possible, and his hair seems blonder than before, exposing his

Nordic heritage. A pure member of the Aryan race. She scoffed to herself.

"I'm fine. Just doing a lot of studying and haven't wanted to be distracted." She lied.

"Say, there's a barbeque on the Fourth of July at a friend's house. There'll be lots of steak and fireworks. We're celebrating. And not just the Fourth. Six of us made the latest cut of candidates for the Moon mission next year. I heard three people from your class will be chosen for the mission as well. They're working on the final selection. How about coming along? It may help you achieve your ambitions to meet these people. Several other astronauts and their families will be there. It'll be fun."

She pondered his words. Of course you made the mission. Should I go? Maybe I'll get a hint who will be selected from my class. I'd kill to find out. I vowed I am finished with men. But, hey, I'll get to meet new people, and I am getting sick of studying and not having any fun. Maybe he's changed. Maybe it will help me to be selected for a mission.

"O.K., I'll go." I can't believe I said that. But maybe it's time to get on with my life. Maybe Steve has changed. It'll be fun to meet some people. I need to think of myself, don't I?

CHAPTER 27
The Barbeque

Wednesday, July 4, 2020, 6:00 p.m., Day 246

"Hi, Joe. I'm glad you could make it. Hey, I like your new, blue Corvette. Come on in and meet everyone."

Joe, relieved he found the mansion belonging to his fellow astronaut and best friend, entered through the solid oak double doors into a cavernous living room filled with people, laughing and talking in groups with music blaring. Beyond the room, multiple, open sliding-glass doors extended the view to grounds surrounding a pool filled with swimmers of all ages. Smoke encircled three grills sending the smell of barbeque through the opening into Joe's nostrils making his hungry.

"I wasn't sure this spread belonged to you, Sam. The directions on my GPS brought me here, but this is a little over-the-top for an astronaut's salary."

"It helps to have a rich bride," laughed Sam. "I'm sorry if it's a little out of the way. But you can't buy a hundred acres close to town. Judging by your new wheels, you're not doing so bad, either." A pretty, petite blond lady walked up to them, and put her arm around Sam. "Honey, how about getting Joe a beer?"

"That would be great, Sandy," Joe shouted after the woman, as she turned and went off to the keg on the patio. She waved back without looking around, acknowledging him. "My new vehicle is a result of a huge contract for my company, Cooper Industries, compliments of our government. I'll take you for a ride, later."

"I hear you have many patents in your name."

"Yes, well, I've been lucky," said Joe.

"It helps to have a one hundred and sixty-four I.Q.," retorted Sam.

"Oh, come on. How did you find that out?" chided Joe.

"Everyone knew that in our dorm at Princeton," Sam answered.

Sandy came back and handed Joe a beer. "Are you two going to stand in the foyer all night? You look hungry, Joe. And you appear to be losing weight. Are you sick?"

"Of course, not, Sandy, I've just been getting a lot of exercise in this regimen we're on," he said trying to sound believable.

"Well, come on, let's fatten you up. It takes a lot of food to keep someone as tall as you healthy. You may be flying to the moon next year, and you'll need your strength. When do they tell you who in your class will be on the mission?"

"I guess some people already know. But they haven't told us, yet. Maybe, somebody knows here. I'll try to squeeze the information out of them."

Sam pointed to the grills outside. "Go get something to eat. That's an order."

Joe saluted, military style, and headed toward the back yard.

****

Sally was getting tired of Steve's medical jokes. She politely listened to one more.

"This old man visits his doctor and after a thorough examination, the doctor tells him, 'I have good news and bad news, what would you like to hear first?'

Patient: Well, give me the bad news first.

Doctor: You have cancer; I estimate that you have about two years left.

Patient: That's terrible! In two years, my life will be over! What kind of good news could you probably tell me, after this?

Doctor: You also have Alzheimer's. In about three months you are going to forget everything I told you."

Everyone laughed except Sally. Steve *had* changed. For the worse.

"Do you want any more Kobe steak?" asked a waiter carrying a plateful of meat.

"No, thank you. But it was delicious. Please tell the chef," Sally entreated to the man.

I thought this would be fun. I guess not.

Sam came over to their table and asked, "Steve would you mind coming into the den and playing a game of billiards with Jack? I've made a bet, that you can beat him, and I don't want you to let me down. Sally, how about if you and the other ladies go swimming? You brought your bathing suit, didn't you?"

"Well, yes, if that's all right, Steve?"

Steve answered, "That's fine. I can beat Jack, any time. Sally, I'll be back in a little while."

Thank God.

The two women and Sally changed into their bathing suits and put their beach towels, provided, on lounge chairs. As they walked over to the poolside, Sally exclaimed, "Last one in is a rotten egg!" All three dove into the turquoise, warm water, laughing as they went.

Sally rose up to the top, lifting her head back as she came out of the water. When she opened her eyes, a shadow loomed over her as the sun lowered in the West. A tall, dark figure stood by the pool and stared at her, legs slightly apart, hands on his hips. He didn't move a muscle. A beach towel hung under his arm that appeared a lot like hers. When her eyes cleared of water, a shock ran through her body, numbing her from her head to her toes.

JOE!

She was speechless.

"Are you having fun?" Joe asked, sarcastically.

"Is your wife here?" retorted Sally.

"I have no wife. I'm divorced. And I've been divorced for two months."

Flustered, Sally swam to the side of the pool. "Could I have my towel, please?"

"Seems like I'm always giving you a towel," he replied as he extended his hand to help her out of the water and put the towel around her shoulders. They walked over and sat down at a table. "Can I get you something to drink?"

"Joe, I'm with someone."

"Doctor Steve Harding? I know. Who do you think set him up to play billiards with Jack?"

"But Sam asked Steve to play with Jack."

"Sam is my best friend from college. He'd do anything for me. By the way, how would you like to fly with me to the moon?"

"Don't be funny. I've heard all the stupid jokes I can handle for one day."

"I'm not joking. You and I have been selected to go as part of the Great Hope Project to the moon next year. Colonel Reilly just informed me."

Sally's voice softened, "Really? But Steve is going. That ought to be interesting."

"I guess you are going to have to make the choice who you want in your life before then, or it could get sticky. We'll be in tight living quarters. Actually, isn't that why you're going to be an astronaut -- to help us all get along?"

"Steve and I have agreed to just be friends. And he's given me no indication to think otherwise. All he cares about is going into space.

"I give Steve more credit than that."

"Credit about what?" Steve said, approaching the couple, and extending his hand to Joe. "Hi. I'm Steve Harding." He turned to Sally. "I made Sam some money. I beat Jack at billiards." He sat down.

"Good for you, Steve," Sally quipped. "Sam could use a little more dough."

Steve studied Joe. "You're one of the new astronauts from the March class, aren't you? What's your name?"

"Yes, I am in the March group. My name's Joe Cooper. We'll be traveling together next year to the Moon."

"Joe Cooper. The inventor and scientist? I didn't recognize you, I'm sorry. You're right. We will be starting training together in the next few months when your class completes basic training."

Sally scowled. They are getting too chummy. This is all I need. "Steve, would you take me home after I change?"

"What about the fireworks? They'll be starting in a few minutes."

Joe grinned at Sally, making her heart flutter. "Yes, Sally. You don't want to miss the fireworks."

Outnumbered, she stood and made her way to the cabana where she changed with the other women.

****

"So what do you think of Sally, Joe?"

Joe studied his adversary. "She is a nice woman, very dedicated, and brilliant in her field." I'm not about to tell you my heart, Stevie boy — that I'm madly in love with her, and want to marry her before our flight in a few months. I think she's the most beautiful woman on Earth, especially in that gorgeous bikini she had on. I about jumped into the pool after her.

"I know all that. I mean how she looked in that swim suit. She's a knock out."

Joe's clenched his fists under the table, as he smiled and added, "Yah, she's hot."

"We used to be engaged. But the opportunity presented itself, and here I am at NASA. You have to keep your priorities straight. I don't think I'll ever get married. There's too many beautiful women who love dating astronauts. Look around us." He waved his arm.

Joe scowled at the blond fool. "And I'm leaving them all for you, my friend." He stood and held out his hand. "See you in training."

"Leaving so soon? Did I say something to offend you?"

"Not at all." He lied. "No, I need to study, and make some phone calls for my business."

"Tonight? On the Fourth of July? What a devoted man. The first year here is a killer, but I understand." He winked at Joe.

Joe winced as he weaved around the crowd toward the door.

"Leaving so soon?"

Joe turned to face Sam. "Ah, yes. This was a bad idea. But I appreciate your efforts, Sam. Now that you and I have reconnected, we'll get together again, soon. I'll call you. Thanks for everything."

****

Sally, dressed with wet, shiny hair pulled back into a pony tail and fresh makeup, came back from the cabana to the table to see Steve by himself.

"Where's your new friend Joe?" she said trying to keep her voice steady while she scanned the crowd.

"He left, leaving you to my lucky self."

Sally's heart sank as the first fireworks exploded.

CHAPTER 28
The Campaign Trail

Thursday, July 5, 2020, 8 a.m. Day 247

"How does your leg feel this morning after being on your feet for so long last night?" Kristen inquired, lowering her husband's newspaper with one hand to serve him a cup of coffee with the other.

Dan gazed at his new bride as she poured the hot liquid into his mug.

"Surprisingly well. The prosthesis feels snug, and this one doesn't rub at all. Dr. Kohl said it fits much better than the last one. The fireworks were great. It says in the Morning News the fundraising dinner raised two-hundred-thousand dollars. We've been lucky. I'm ahead by ten percent in the state polls."

"I have no doubt I will be the wife of a Texas Congressman this November," she replied smiling. "Coming to the Rosewood was brilliant, darling. If the campaign trail makes us too busy to have a real honeymoon, it helps to stay in a five-star hotel here in Dallas. My next appointment is at noon. I know you have meetings this morning. But I'm going to get a massage and make a trip to the pool before I get ready for the Ladies' Luncheon. It will be heavenly. Thank you for making all the arrangements. You will make a great President someday."

Dan put his hand over hers. "One step at a time, sweetheart. One step at a time."

CHAPTER 29
Anniversary

Sunday, October 28, 2020, 8:00 a.m. Day 365

The anniversary of the Impact Event began with many memorials and remembrances planned all over the world.

Sally turned off the news on her laptop, set down her orange juice glass, and wiped her mouth with her pajama sleeve. She leaned her head back against the chair returning to her studies, once again, and tried to concentrate on the specifications of the J-2X engine being used in the Aries rocket that would propel her and five other astronauts to the Moon.

Failing in her concentration, she stood, moved to the window and studied the rain, watching beads of water slide down the glass. The brown leaves fell one by one to the ground. Texas Octobers couldn't compete with the colorful fall season in New York. The morning vision matched her mood. Her brain overflowed with thoughts of Joe, wondering if he studied or slept on this melancholy Sunday. Was he alone? She couldn't believe a year had passed since they met at the Fresno airport.

Now, their grueling study schedules made it impossible to talk to each other— or so she surmised. A simple nod was her sole acknowledgment when she smiled at him in the hall or cafeteria. With one on one instruction, they did not interact. When they shared classes, he kept to himself.

Has he forgotten about me?

She had not spoken to Steve in three months, after telling him at the barbeque there was nothing left between them, and their relationship would be strictly friends. She knew now, only Joe mattered now. He was divorced, and she must find a way back into his heart.

****

Joe enjoyed running in the rain. He felt a part of the elements. It kept him cool. But not today. Like always, thoughts of Sally burned through him. Thinking of her in Steve's arms drove him crazy. He ran faster. But in the end, after ten miles, he stopped in front of the Landings Coffee Shop and walked in. It was the anniversary of the meteorite plunging into the Earth, changing the direction of the world and his life, forever. The flat screen on the wall showed President Vail laying a wreath in a park in San Jose´ to commemorate those lost in the Impact Event. The memorial was one of many under construction, or planned, around the circumference of ground zero.

Why did she always smile at him? Must be her form of torture. He couldn't take much more. And next week the hands-on training for the mission would begin. How would he endure seeing them together? Maybe he should opt out of the program and concentrate on his company back in Los Angeles.

Am I crazy? Why should I do that when I have my business manager, Dick, to handle decisions while I'm gone? Hasn't he already made me rich?

No. I've wanted this opportunity all my life, and no woman is going to ruin my career to explore the cosmos.

CHAPTER 30
Training

Monday, November 5, 2020 8:00 a.m. Day 373

"Good morning, astronauts."

Sally viewed Samuel Cooke, their instructor, and former crew member of many former missions. An authority on the *Aries I* rocket that would escort them to low Earth orbit and the *Orion* spacecraft, their transport to the Moon, he would give them an overview of the vehicle and explain their missions.

"Good morning," she answered in unison with the other five, crew members.

Rigid and afraid to turn around in the small classroom, Sally felt the presence of the two former men in her life. Arriving first, she entered the door at the back of the room, making her way to sit in the front seat, she couldn't see either one, but sensed eyes burning through her. How was this all going to work? How ironic that she lived her dream to be part of a space mission crew, only to have two of the crewmembers be Steve and Joe. Was she up for the challenge?

****

In the frontal lobe of his mind, Joe heard Dr. Cooke explaining the diagram of the *Orion* spacecraft layout. But with his occipital cortex, he stared at the auburn tresses flowing down Sally's back. Beautiful, he thought. No. No. No. Stop thinking about her. If this mission is going to be possible, he had to forget their brief courtship and settle down to the business of learning about the spacecraft that would be their ride to the Moon. She was another man's woman.

****

Sally and Joe turned their attention to the instructor. For the next two hours the six astronauts learned about the *Aries I* and the modified *Orion* Spacecraft.

"The *Orion* capsule," Colonel Cooke expounded, "has been overhauled and two additional crewmembers can now be accommodated. Although the space is limited, the short, three-day trek to the Moon should be tolerable. When you land, equipment previously delivered by the Aries V and an unmanned spacecraft will await you. It will be your mission to assemble the parts to make a habitat for future astronauts. The habitat will be capable of supporting life for six people, for a duration of four months."

"It will take you three to four weeks to complete the mission. Stan will be Commander of the flight. He has three missions under his belt, and knows as much about your vehicle as I do. Bruce will be second-in-command and will be co-pilot. Joe, your expertise in physics and engineering will be invaluable to assembling the Moon living quarters. Your helper will be Gretchen, who has admirable credentials in electrical and chemical engineering. Steve will be the medical specialist if needed, and will perform experiments he is preparing. Sally, you will keep everyone sane, and conduct experiments on long-term, close quarter habitation. This information will be vital for our future trips. As you know, the Space Program has been accelerated tremendously. The Constellation Program has been renewed. Your training for the expedition will be condensed to three months. Normally, it takes a year. This is why we have chosen people of your stature to accomplish these objectives. Do you think you are all up to it?'

Everyone nodded.

"Good. If there are no *Quest*ions, we'll take a break. Be back here in fifteen minutes."

Everyone stood.

Sally mustered all the courage she could, and turned slowly around. Joe stared at her momentarily, said hello, and walked past her toward Dr. Cooke.

Deflated, she nodded to Steve who talked to Gretchen. In the hallway, the voices grew faint as she moved toward the lavatory. Hope that Joe would follow her dissipated with the lack of footsteps. She stepped through the door marked WOMEN.

Disappointment filled her, and her eyes welled and her shoulders slumped. He didn't care for her, any more. She grabbed a tissue off the sink, wiped her eyes and blew her nose. Exiting the bathroom, she bought a soda in the drink machine and walked back to the room. Chin up and without turning her head, she walked back to her seat and sat down. I am giving all my energies to the mission. Love will have to wait.

CHAPTER 31
We Have Lift Off

Tuesday, January 15, 2019 12:39 p.m., Enroute to Moon

"T minus ten. Nine. Eight."

Sally's fingers tingled as the countdown reached the last few seconds. Strapped into her seat, space suit on, her heart pounded and her head throbbed with excitement.

"Seven.

"Six.

"Five.

"Four."

This is it. My training is over and this is the real thing!

"Three.

"Two.

"One."

The roar of the engines was deafening. The vibration rattled her brain. And then she felt movement of the missile upward. Her gut pulled, and she felt suspended in time.

This is actually happening!

"Lift off! We have lift off," announced mission control in her headset.

The *Aries I*, with its 3.6 million pounds of thrust, rose into the air carrying its payload, including six human beings packed inside the *Orion* capsule hooked to the nose.

Sally heard Captain Stan say, "All systems are go." Her only job at this point of the flight consisted of sitting still and keeping quiet.

She lay on her back, as they were thrust upward toward the heavens accelerating above one thousand miles per hour, thinking about Joe, strapped in his space suit next to her — their destinies joined for four months. She couldn't see him, but sensed his presence and his nearness making her shiver inside. The computer panels above her showed a steady green on the gauges, indicating the launch was a "Go."

"T plus 20 seconds."

As mission control spoke, Sally felt the missile roll 180 degrees to a 78 degrees' pitch attitude.

"T plus 2 minutes."

The solid rocket boosters and fuel tank are separating from the orbiter. We are at twenty- eight miles from the lift-off sight. Sally mentally recalled her diligent studying of the launch process. The main engines are still firing.

Once again mission control filled her helmet with its voice. "T plus 8.5 minutes." Captain Stan confirmed the shutdown of the main engines.

Finally, after more transmissions and responses from the captain, the orbital maneuvering systems fired. We're about 250 miles above the Earth, at circular orbit, placing us into high orbit. We're on our way to the Moon!

****

During the flight, the seats folded into the wall area to gain access to compartments located under them. The space-suits came off and the crew proceeded to carry out their mission objectives for the enroute flight.

Sally enjoyed the weightless condition floating to accomplish inflight duties assigned to her. Controlling her emotions by keeping busy, she wrote reports of the activities of the crew members, recording into a computer sleep habits and apparent mental attitudes of each of the five others. Everyone, on the outside, remained professional for the time being. Her butterflies, caused by the nearness of Joe, faded with his stoic responses to the mission-related *Quest*ions she asked. As the Moon grew larger and the Earth grew smaller, the six settled into their daily routine. When three slept, three remained awake tending to the chores at hand. Time passed quickly.

****

Joe was baffled. As he checked the oxygen supply, he couldn't help but wonder if Sally and Steve were back together why didn't they talk more to each other? And Steve constantly flirted with Gretchen. It didn't make any sense. It killed him to act so indifferent to interactions with Sally. But he had his pride.

****

On the third day, Captain Stan maneuvered *Orion* into low lunar orbit. Here, the spacecraft would stay, controlled remotely by Houston, as the astronauts boarded the lander module, named *Quest*. This vehicle, attached to the nose of Orion, would be their transportation to the surface of the Moon and back again after four months.

Gretchen, the expert on the systems of *Quest*, opened the adjoining latch, and crawled through to the dark vehicle. With flashlight in hand, she awakened the lander by starting its auxiliary power unit. Suddenly, it filled with light. She turned on the computers. She announced through their modified space suits, the rest could board. One by one, the remaining crew entered the lander and strapped into their seats. Captain Stan used his hand held "mouse" to program the computers for landing. Joe, the last astronaut to enter *Quest*, closed and locked the hatch. When each announced to Stan they were ready, Stan disengaged the lander and started the engines.

The landing sequence began.

"Houston, this is Captain Stan. We're GO for landing."

"Roger, Stan. You look good from mission control."

The module slowed as it neared the Moon's surface.

"600-feet, down 19," stated Stan.

And thirty seconds later, "300 feet, down 3 ½, 47 forward."

"40-feet, down 2 ½. Kicking up some dust."

Sally did not understand the call-outs Captain Stan made to Houston.

Again, she sat in her space suit getting butterflies in her stomach. She had no duties to perform during this time. She thought about Joe. What is he thinking? Surely not about me. Maybe about someone else? Inside her helmet her eyes welled.

I can't cry while I'm landing on the Moon!

At last, the *Orion* crew felt a bump.

Then came the words everyone held their breath to hear, "Contact light. We have touch down. *Quest* has landed."

The crew heard the clapping and shouting at mission control in Houston.

Sally exhaled. I don't believe it. I'm on the Moon!

CHAPTER 32
Missing

Thursday, January 17, 2021, 4:29 p.m., Day 446, Moon

Steve scowled. "I don't remember this Extravehicular Mobility Unit being so tight!" Entering the spacewalk suit from the rear proved difficult for him, but would allow him to survive outside the lunar lander for eight hours or 480 minutes. It provided pressurization, oxygen, water, temperature control, and carbon dioxide removal.

Bruce, a smaller man than Steve's six-foot-three stature at five-foot-ten, had more luck, and donned his in five minutes. Sally fastened the closures on the suits, amazed at the technology involved with these EMUs.

Gretchen opened the hatch to the airlock. Once in, with the inner hatch locked, the chamber acclimated to the outside, and the two men exited *Quest* through the outer door onto the lunar surface.

Steve scanned the terrain to find the Rover, a lunar roving vehicle, LRV, dropped previously, along with other supplies, by four unmanned landers.

Bruce spotted it first, hopping in the low gravity, making footprints on the dusty ground as he approached. The two men climbed aboard the two-seater vehicle. A flatbed made up the rear to transport the supplies necessary to build a permanent habitat.

Bruce installed the battery, previously charged on *Quest*. It started on the first try. After two hours, they had gathered most of the supplies.

They communicated to the lander and each other with radios in their space helmets. At the gathering station, Bruce jumped off the Rover and began sorting the materials.

"Steve, I don't see the box of tools, critical to assemble our habitat. Would you try to pick up a tracking signal and find it?"

"Sure. I'll look around."

"I believe the box is yellow," added Bruce, as Steve sped away.

Thirty minutes later, Bruce called his partner. "Steve, have you found the tool box?"

No answer.

"Steve, do you hear me?" Bruce asked again.

No answer.

Concerned, Bruce inquired, "*Quest*. Do you read me?"

"Loud and clear, Bruce. How me?" asked Stan.

"Have you heard any transmissions from Steve? I can't seem to reach him."

"No, I haven't," replied Stan. "His radio must have malfunctioned."

"Yah. Well, I'll look around. How about if you scan the area with your binoculars and let me know if you see the Rover?"

"Will do. Then I need to tell Houston," answered the captain.

Two minutes passed. "Bruce, Stan. I don't see the Rover or Steve. I will declare a Code Yellow and alert Houston. I'll also try to pick up the Rover's transponder on the computer."

"Roger," answered Bruce. "And I'll attempt to follow the maze of tracks left by Rover."

The announcement Steve was missing sent chills through Sally. Although she knew how risky the whole mission could be, she always tried to focus on the positive.

Steve is missing.

Suddenly, the reality of the situation hit her. She now existed over two hundred thousand miles from Earth, in a space capsule that barely accommodated six people. And I can't dial 911.

Steve — what if they didn't find him? I don't love him anymore, but he is part of my crew and my past.

A familiar voice entered her awareness. "Sally. Would you help me with my EMU? I'm needed out there." Joe stared straight into Sally's eyes. Can he see inside me? Is he reading my mind?

"Ah. Of course," Oh no. I might lose him too, and I couldn't bear it. Maybe I don't have the "right stuff" to be an astronaut.

She gulped a big breath and tried to stop shaking. As she fumbled with his moon walking suit, his nearness made her heart beat faster, and she tried to compose herself. All hope would be gone if anything happens to him. Once again, their eyes met, and his lips parted as if to speak. And then, he took his helmet and quickly floated to the portal.

"Be safe," Sally whispered. He must have heard, because without speaking, he raised his arm in response and exited.

CHAPTER 33
Found

Thursday, January 17,2021, 7:40 p.m., Day 446, Moon

Joe climbed down the steps of *Quest*, careful not to snag a hole in his EMU. As he jumped down the last foot to the dusty surface, he wondered why Sally seemed so nervous when she helped him don his space suit. Is it possible she still has feelings for me? Or was I imagining the look in her eye? Maybe Steve is the one she worries about.

Pushing the thoughts out of his mind, he focused on finding Steve. Weighing 16.5% of what his Earth weight measured, he easily spanned the distance to where he spotted Bruce studying his transponder.

"Are you picking up a signal?" Joe asked the second-in-command when he reached him.

"Yes," Bruce answered. He lifted his head momentarily, and pointed his finger to his left. "It's coming from that direction." He pressed his intercom button. "Stan, do you concur?"

"Yes," answered the Commander from inside *Quest*. "I'll give you directions as you go."

Joe hopped over to Bruce. "Here. Let me put this fresh battery and oxygen unit on you."

"Good thinking," said Bruce.

Unit changed, Joe suggested they follow the tracks made by the Rover when Steve rounded up the supplies. But tracks were everywhere and led in all directions, overlapping and weaving over each other. The two men followed the signal until pristine tracks led them farther and farther away from *Quest*.

The rim of a crater loomed ahead. It proved to be farther than reality, and took several minutes to reach the edge. The tracks of the Rover led directly to the brim. They scanned the deep hole. Peering down into the shadows, Joe surmised it must be about one hundred-feet deep.

"Stan, we're at the edge of a crater. Can you pull up the map on the computer and tell us how big this thing is? If it's not too deep, we need to get down there. It looks like Steve went over the edge with the Rover."

"Oh no! I'll look it up stat," answered Stan.

Both men scanned the deep hole with their search lights. At first, they didn't see anything. Then Bruce spotted the back of the Rover angled down into a crevice.

"I see the Rover! It's upside down," shouted Bruce. "But I don't see Steve. We have to get down there. He must have been thrown from the vehicle."

Stan interjected, "The ravine is a meteorite impact area. The circumference of the hole is a little over one-hundred-feet across, and seventy-two-feet down to the bottom."

"We have a rappelling rope in our cache," said Bruce. "I need to get it."

Seeing no other option, Joe nodded. "Hurry," he replied. "Steve must be hurt bad."

As Bruce hopped away, Joe circled the crater, trying to analyze the best place to descend. He called to Steve using the transmitters they all shared, but received no reply.

Fleeting through his mind, the thought that Steve might be out of the picture for good wormed its way into his consciousness. But he dismissed it immediately. He never wanted Steve dead.

After seven minutes, Bruce appeared carrying the rappelling rope.

"I scouted the rim, and I think we need to climb down over there about twenty yards."

Bruce pounded the stake into the ground and tied a double figure eight knot through the carabiner. Joe linked the rappelling equipment to his harness fitted over his space suit. Finished, he leaned back and slowly let the rope go through his gloved hands while he bounced against the rock face of the crater and rappelled down to the bottom. In the past, he rappelled and loved it, not knowing he'd one day be using it to save a person's life.

Finally, he reached the bottom and detached himself from the rope. Bruce told him the transponder on the Rover sounded close to Joe's position.

Boulders, fallen from the rim made it hard to see, even with his lantern.

He circled around several, until there, a few yards away, he saw the damaged Rover, mangled.

All personal feelings aside, Joe leaped to the Rover to find and help Steve. But his rival was nowhere to be seen. He bent down and peered under the Rover. There, the grim reality surfaced.

Steve, with a large opening in his spacesuit, lay dead.

Joe's stomach lurched. Steve either suffocated or died, instantly, crushed by the Rover. He didn't suffer.

His thoughts turned to Sally. Would she be devastated? Would she be able to carry on with the mission? What choice did she have? He needed to tell everyone.

"Bruce? Stan? I found Steve. He didn't make it. He's dead."

CHAPTER 34
No Time to Grieve

Thursday, January 31, 2019, 2:00 p.m., EST, Moon

Two weeks passed since Steve's death. After consulting NASA, the decision was made to leave Steve's body in the crater. The effort to move the Rover, to free Steve's body, could endanger the remaining crew, and use precious oxygen and time. Joe pounded a cross into the Moon's surface at the point Steve went over the cliff, in his memory, and they held a brief memorial service in the capsule. But afterwards, by necessity, they all returned to the mission at hand.

Sally dealt with her grief by writing on the computer detailed accounts of each one of the crew's reactions to the tragedy. Analyzing her own feelings, she typed that she handled losing him quite well. She didn't shed any tears, and found working helped. Talking to the rest of the crew cemented the realization that they had critical jobs to do. Feelings must be controlled, and their workloads all increased as they filled the void created by Steve's absence.

In addition, she worked other jobs. She emptied the toilet, prepared meals, and continued to help the spacewalkers into their EMUs. She did not leave *Quest*. Stan also remained in the space module. At times she felt a little claustrophobic, but remedied it by closing her eyes for a few moments. She couldn't wait for the completion of the habitat.

Gretchen, in charge of building the structure, spent most of her hours outside *Quest*, attaching blocks like a Lego set, routing electrical wires, and fitting plumbing. She explained building the unit resembled putting a puzzle together. All parts had markings, so Part A went into Part B, and so on. Sally wrote how much the lady engineer loved her job.

Bruce, in addition to being second-in-command as a pilot of *Quest*, provided his expertise, drawing knowledge from a doctorate degree in mechanical engineering. He helped Gretchen assemble the habitat, gluing the bundles of tubing and attaching sheets of a special foam material to the assembled tubes.

Joe, the expert on providing a livable environment in the biosphere being constructed, took his turns outside *Quest*. He spent his days insuring the quality of the life-supporting atmosphere inside their space capsule, as well as hooking up the generators and equipment that would run the environmental systems of the habitat.

Working fourteen hours each day, left no time for Sally and Joe to converse on a personal level. Their conversations were totally professional.

Finally, on February 5, Gretchen announced to the crew the habitat was completed. The message to Houston Mission Control resulted in resounding cheers and the news spread around the world.

Sally held her breath when the generator switches were turned on. They worked. And suddenly, peering through a portal of *Quest*, she saw light fill the structure they nicknamed the "Igloo," after its shape and white color.

February sixth became moving day. This time, Sally donned an EMU helped by Gretchen and entered the airlock. With the air sucked out, she opened the hatch. Joe came out behind her.

Sally climbed down the steps and turned around. Her mouth dropped open as she scanned the surface and horizon with wonder. There, bathed in light and suspended in space, Earth hung before her like a giant blue and white marble. She gasped at the beauty.

Joe jumped off the last step of *Quest* and hopped up beside her.

"Quite a sight, isn't it?"

Sally turned slightly to view Joe's face through his head gear. He grinned. She couldn't decide which display offered the most beauty. His smile, or the Earth.

His smile, of course. But I've lost him. Eyebrows furrowed, she headed for the Igloo leaving Joe staring at her.

****

Once inside, Bruce, Joe and Gretchen checked all the systems to ensure it was safe to take their EMUs off.

Gretchen read the computer indicators. "Oxygen levels … green. Temperature 70 degrees. Pressure levels … green. Everything appears normal. Sally, would you be first to take your EMU off?"

"Sure," Sally replied, trying not to seem nervous. She trusted the scientists turned astronauts, but she couldn't help the butterflies that stirred in her belly.

As Joe unzipped her spacesuit, Sally took a big breath. Which is more unnerving? Dying? Or Joe unzipping my outfit? She stepped back out of her EMU, still alive.

"I'm good. The air smells like insulation and leather, but I can breathe fine. The temperature is comfortable. The pressure feels normal...for the Moon." She grinned.

"O.K., everyone, EMUs off," Bruce commanded.

Joe turned to Sally. "It's your turn to undress me."

Sally said, "Turn around." Unzipping him was unnerving. Why does he have this effect on me?

Bruce made the announcement to Stan who waited anxiously in *Quest* for the announcement that they were a "go" in the Igloo.

"You are the first folks to inhabit a domicile on the Moon, even if it is for only two days," jested Stan.

Bruce added to his roommates, "He's right. We have two days to check that everything works, right down to the food heater and the commode."

Sally thought the Igloo spacious compared to *Quest*. They spread out, and began to labor at their predesignated duties exercised many times in training.

While eating at the table that evening, Joe and Sally both reached for a packet of coffee at the same time, resulting in their hands touching. Startled, Sally blushed and Joe left his hand over hers for more than three seconds. Sally went crazy inside.

"Sorry," quipped Joe, not taking his eyes off of her face.

Sally stared back in an eye lock. "There's more than one packet of coffee."

"I want this one," retorted Joe.

What is wrong with him? What is wrong with me? Sally's mind whirled.

She let go, pulling her hand out from under his. "Have it then, but it has what I like in it," she said, giving up.

Joe said nothing, as he moved to the hot water dispenser. When the packet was full he returned to the table. Holding it out, he said, "It is yours. I just wanted to fix it for you."

"Oh. Well, thanks." What is happening? Was that a come-on? No. Couldn't be.

Everyone finished their meals. Sally had chicken with rice. Bruce had beef stew. Joe and Gretchen had rice and beans. All the food came in ready-made packets. They all agreed the food proved to be pretty good as well as nutritious.

At ten o'clock they crawled into bunks lining one side of the Igloo.

"Good night, everyone," Bruce chimed. "This has been a momentous day. Sleep well. We have a lot to do, tomorrow."

"Good night, Bruce," said Gretchen.

"Good night, Bruce," said Sally.

"Good night, Sally," said Joe.

Sally coughed. "Good night." He's up to something, but he's too chicken to be out with it.

****

The next two days were spent testing all the equipment in the Igloo. Gretchen and Bruce spent time outside the new building cleaning up and piling the tools and extra parts into neat rows, so the next travelers could use them as needed. Sally completed her log and commentary. She wrote that she felt comfortable and safe in the habitat, and decided she wouldn't mind coming back to stay for an extended period of time.

By the third day, they were up at six o'clock a.m. Today they departed for Earth. As Sally approached the hatch, she turned around and scanned the interior of the Igloo for the last time, so she wouldn't forget it. Outside, they bounced their way to *Quest* to prepare for their blast off to rendezvous with the Orion.

"Hello," Stan offered to each one as they took turns climbing through the hatch and into the space capsule. "It's good to see you all once again. How was your stay in the Igloo?"

"It was awesome," replied Joe. "Everything works. Houston will be very pleased."

Strapping into their seats for lift off, Joe stood next to Sally. He reached for her arm. Startled, she lifted her face to gaze into his smoky green eyes.

He spoke. "When we get back to Earth, we're going to have a long talk."

CHAPTER 35
The Talk

Friday, February 22, 2021, 5:00 p.m.,
Johnson Space Center, Houston

"You walk too fast; you know that?" Joe shouted, out of breath. "Wait up!"

"I'm trying to get away from you as quickly as I can," retorted Sally, half-heartedly.

She stopped and waited for him.

"I've been trying to talk to you ever since we returned from the Moon, but you keep getting away from me." He caught up to her. "Where did you take off to when you got back? I haven't been able to find you since our debriefings over a week ago."

"I flew to Denver to see Jeannie, my cousin."

"Well. You are not getting away from me this time. I haven't been able to call you since you changed your phone number. And it's unlisted. What's up with you, anyway? You used to be so gregarious."

"I still like people. I have simply been avoiding SOME people."

"And would that some people be me? At least you're honest."

"Look. I'm freezing out here. Let's get a cup of coffee at Bud's Café."

Once inside the warm cafe´, Joe pulled a chair out for Sally, and she sat down.

"Remember when we used to come here after classes?" Joe asked.

"Of course, Joe. Please what did you want to talk about?"

"First of all, I want to apologize for not telling you I was married. We were legally separated, but I know I should have told you."

"Yes. You should have. Do you have any idea what that did to me? It crushed me. I never thought my heart would get broken twice."

"I have been trying to make it up to you for over a year, now, but you won't give me a chance. I want to tell you something before you get up and walk away, again, like you did at the barbeque. I was upset when I saw you with Steve. But I don't blame you. I blame me. If I would have been honest from the start, this would never have happened.

Sally, I have to tell you, I am in love with you. In a way I have never loved anyone. You mean more to me than any-thing, and I want you to give me another chance. Would you?"

Sally almost swooned. I'm going to float if I don't hold on to my chair. Could this be true? Of course it is. He just said it!

"Yes, I will. But don't you ever lie to me, again, do you hear me?"

"Yes, I hear you."

They finished their coffee and talked about their selection to the Mars Project and the studying they would do together before training started March 27th.

When they finished their coffee, they stepped back out into the brisk, February air. Joe turned to Sally.

"I am parked down the street. Would you like to see my apartment? I am having it redecorated and it would be great if you could give me some advice."

"I'd love to. We can come back and get my car, later."

"Much later," Joe said as he opened the door to his Corvette.

CHAPTER 36
Commitment

Wednesday, May 15, 2021, 7:15 p.m., Houston

The doorbell rang and Sally glanced in the hall mirror to make a last minute check. Joe was right on time, as usual. The smell of flowers filled the room. A card that said: Happy Birthday, all my love, Joe, came with them, and the gorgeous bouquet now filled a vase on her coffee table.

Joe told her to dress up because he had a special evening planned for her. She hoped he would like the emerald green dress she bought. She loved the color and it went with her auburn hair. Satisfied with her appearance, she opened the door. One problem remained… her birthday was December 2nd. What could he be up to?

Joe whistled at her and raised his eyebrows. "You are the most beautiful creature I have ever seen. I don't often see you wearing makeup. You look great! Happy Birthday."

"There's one thing you need to know, Joe. It's not my birthday.

"I know, but I am making up for all the ones I missed. So, I am taking you out on the town, tonight, my dear. Your chariot awaits."

Pulling the door behind her, they took the elevator to the first floor and made their way to his car.

She lowered her head as he held the door and she swept her dress into the small vehicle. Her head almost reached the ceiling.

"You must be doing well, to have a new Corvette," she said smiling.

"My business is doing well in California. I have a great manager and financial advisor." He smiled back.

"So. Where are you taking me?"

"First, we are going to dinner at *La Fleure*."

"Wow, that's a five-star restaurant. I'm flattered."

When they arrived at the nightclub, the valet parked the car, and they went inside. Water trickled down the rocks of a fountain in the center of the room making musical sounds, while a piano could be heard in the dining room.

"We have reservations," offered Joe as he approached the podium.

"Name?" asked the waiter.

"Cooper. Joe Cooper."

"Ah, yes, Doctor Joe Cooper. Yes, sir, right this way. We have a special table for you in our Valentine Room."

Joe put his hand under Sally's arm and led her behind the waiter around many tables in the dining room to the back of the main room. There was not an empty table. The waiter held open a door, and Joe and Sally walked into a private area shaped like a heart. The floor had dark red carpeting. The lone table in the middle of the 12-feet by 12-feet room stood below a crystal chandelier. The piano music filtered in through the sound system on the ceiling. Sitting, the waiter handed the couple menus, as another filled their water glasses.

"You picked a pretty fancy place to dine, Joe," said Sally as she reached over and put her hand over his, smiling.

"Nothing but the best for my favorite, birthday girl."

After a dinner of prime rib, and all the trimmings, Joe announced, "I have a present for you."

"All this, is present enough," said Sally waving her hand. "How can you top this?"

He pulled out a tiny package. "Maybe with this." He handed her the small wrapped present.

As she opened it, tears began to well in her eyes, anticipating the obvious. When she flipped open the velvet box, a two-carat diamond ring sparkled up at her.

He rounded the table and knelt down on one knee.

"Sally I have waited for this day for two years… Will you marry me?"

Sally's heart beat fast and she began shaking. "Of course, I'll marry you. I can't believe it. I can't believe it. We will be husband and wife on Mars."

CHAPTER 37
Plans for Survivors

Wednesday, March 6, 2021, 6:15 p.m. Day 494

"Melissa eat your supper," the First Lady of the United States coaxed, as her twelve-year old daughter scowled.

The door to the private family dining room swung open.

"Oh good, you made it," exclaimed the President's wife. Her husband pecked her on the cheek and smiled widely at his daughter.

When Melissa saw her father, her unhappy face now beamed. "Thank you for making it to sing "Happy Birthday" and blow out my candles, Daddy, I didn't think you would make it."

President Vail sat down next to his daughter and wrapped his arms around her. "I wouldn't miss it for the world. Literally." He winked at the First Lady.

"How did your day go? Did you meet with the astronauts?"

"Yes. And both, Joe Cooper and Sally Richards, agreed to be on the maiden voyage to Mars next year." He tried to appear jovial for his daughter's birthday, but it had been a rough day.

"That's great, dear. Did you read in the papers that Joe and Sally are engaged?"

"Yes. I knew that. Congressman Dan Alexander told me at our meeting, yesterday. Do you know, I think, if he were older, he'd be running against me for my job. He has a good future in politics."

The dining room door leading to the kitchen opened, and Louise, the main chef, walked into the dining room carrying a fourteen-inch-round ice-cream cake with twelve lighted candles surrounding a picture of Justin Bieber, the singing heart throb. The rest of the kitchen staff followed her in and gathered around Melissa.

The President moved to the table's head and began to sing "Happy Birthday" to his daughter.

At the end of the song, Melissa tried to blow out the candles. They stayed lit.

"Blow out your candles, honey," said the Commander in Chief grinning.

"They won't blow out," laughed Melissa. After a third try, Louise chuckling, admitted the mischievous deed in putting special candles that would not blow out on the cake.

"Is the surprise ready?" Asked the President.

"Yes, sir."

"Well, bring it in."

The side door swung open, and a bell, attached to a new, red bicycle, started ringing. Lee, an aide, sat on it and rode it around the room to Melissa's chair. The young girl jumped up and as Lee demounted, Melissa climbed on. Out through the doors she went flying, and into the large hall.

When she came back, she ran up to her mom and dad shouting, "This is the best birthday I ever had!"

"And may you have many more, sweetheart," said the President as he frowned thinking about new information on the impending collision with multi-asteroid remnants and their looming disaster in 2058.

****

Later, with Melissa in bed, the President and his wife, sat on the couch in their living quarters. They were alone.

"I haven't seen you smile since you gave the bike to Melissa. Is something wrong that you can talk about?"

The President said, "Let's go to our room. This is extremely confidential."

In their bedroom, the First Lady said, "What is it?"

"In thirty-seven years, I'll be seventy-nine years old. But Melissa will only be forty-nine."

"You can add… So?"

"Darling. It's not only because a large meteor hit San Francisco that we are expanding the Space Program. There is another more critical reason."

"Go on."

The President noticed goose bumps on his wife's arms.

"As you know, the asteroid, Seriod, broke up last year, causing a rogue meteor to hit the Earth. This disaster isn't the only reason the world's leaders decided to cooperate and join our efforts in establishing a Moon and Mars colony.

There is a colossal debris field orbiting the sun. In the year 2056, Earth's orbit has a 99.9 percent chance of crossing the paths of at least one or several of these fragments. Previously, the scientists thought we could handle the small ones expected. Now, we know several could collide with the Earth. Some are a half a mile in diameter, which is about the size of the meteorite that killed the dinosaurs. All the re-nowned scientists of the world have agreed to these findings. I received the briefing, today. The Earth will be changed for thousands of years.

You and I will be getting old, then. But Melissa will still have many years to live. We must get colonies estab-lished in other parts of the solar system. We have the tech-nology. The world leaders have collaborated and the effort is being accelerated in all countries with a space program. We hope that by 2058, we will have thirteen colonies, self-contained in outer space. Next month, the Russians will land near our habitat on the Moon and live there for several months.

In a year, we will build another habitat on Mars. Sup-plies will soon be delivered near one of the poles of the plan-et, where plentiful water is thought to exist under a thin car-bon dioxide crust. Joe and Sally will stay indefinitely on Mars. They will be continually supplied with necessities un-til they are self-supporting, which may take two years. Many other astronauts have committed to the Program, and will emigrate when feasible."

The First Lady wrung her hands. "Are you saying you want Melissa to live on one of these colonies?"

"Yes. You are intuitive. I'm hoping she will be a survi-vor. Joe and Sally are going to try to have children on Mars. Maybe Melissa will, too."

"And us?"

"The Earth may never recover. I will always be Mr. President. It carries many privileges. We will spend an un-known amount of time underground. Plans are already in action. There are miles of caves in the Midwest salt mines. They are being prepared as I speak. If we don't take a direct hit, we should survive."

The First Lady stared at the blue carpet, her eyes welling. "Surely, we will be able to do something. What about a shield? Or weapons? Who knows what we'll have by then?"

"Yes. There are those possibilities. And we're working on all options, most definitely. But we can't count on them. The brightest minds are working on all solutions."

President Vail put his hands on his wife's shoulders and tried to comfort her. In his mind he prayed she was right.

CHAPTER 38
Wedding Bells

Saturday, September 7, 2021, 1:15 p.m., Day 679 Houston

"Does anyone know where my earrings are?" the bride chimed.

"Here they are darling," answered Beverly, Sally's excited mom. "You look beautiful."

Sally studied herself in the ceiling to floor mirror as she poked the solitaire diamond studs through her ears, a gift from Joe. Dressed for her own wedding in the Riverside Church's Bridal Preparation Room, she was satisfied she and Joe had opted for a small thirty-invitation wedding. Tall, toned from all the physical workouts, and slim, she approved of the fitted, satin floor-length gown her mother and she had picked out. She reached up and straightened the tiara from which hung a short chin length veil and licked her finger to tame a rogue hair strand. Excitement made her fingers tingle as she clutched her bouquet of Forget Me Nots, her favorite flowers.

Her matron of honor, Jeannie, nodded her approval as Sally winked at her cousin.

She jolted as the quiet church's organ suddenly began playing the musical notes of a preselected favorite song, Just the Way You Are.

"Our cue," said Jeannie, smiling. "It's time."

"I can't breathe," uttered Sally.

"It's probably because that dress is so tight," laughed her mother.

"Oh, Mom, it's the style."

"Let's go. Your soon-to-be husband is waiting."

Sally, her mom and Jeannie, moved to the rear of the sanctuary, as the organ began playing the Bridal Chorus by Wagner.

Sally's father, George, offered his arm, and soon she walked toward Joe, staring at her in the front of the church.

He is the most handsome man on Earth, thought Sally, as she struggled to keep her eyes from welling. Please don't let me forget my vows.

The Baptist preacher waited until Sally reached the altar and then began the ceremony.

Sally and Joe declared their vows and exchanged rings. When the pastor said, you are man and wife and you may kiss the bride, Joe grinned and gave Sally a prolonged kiss that made the witnesses present laugh and applaud.

Sam, the best man, congratulated the newly married couple, as Joe took Sally's arm and walked her toward the back of the church to form a receiving line.

Sally couldn't believe her new name had just become Sally Cooper.

No time to have off from their grueling schedules of training for the next mission, their honeymoon would be on Mars.

CHAPTER 39
Enroute to Mars

Sunday, August 30, 2022, 7:00 a.m.
Earth time EDT, Enroute to Mars

"Sally, wake up. Come look at the view."

The lady astronaut stretched and yawned. Unzipping her pod, she floated over to where Joe peered out the foot-square window, encircling him with her arms as she gazed. Mars loomed ahead and the panorama took Sally's breath away.

"You sure know how to pick a place for a postponed honeymoon," she whispered in his ear.

"Only the best for you, my love."

Sally turned from the portal, back to her new husband.

"I can't believe we have been traveling five and a half months. I think it's gone pretty fast."

"That's because we've been so busy."

"I didn't imagine I would like horticulture," Sally remarked. "But it's exciting to see the plants growing. The tomatoes will be bearing fruit in three weeks. We'll be eating fresh vegetables in our home on the red planet. I'm excited. It'll beat packaged food."

"We're real-life pioneers, Sally. Are you having any second thoughts?"

"Absolutely not. I've been preparing for this for years. How about you?"

"As long as you are here, I don't need the other eight billion humans to keep me happy."

Sally smiled, pulled him close, and gave him a loving hug. "We need to get dressed. The other four are already eating breakfast."

Then they heard a loud thump and the space vehicle shuddered.

CHAPTER 40
Communications Lost

Sunday, August 30, 2022, 9:08 a.m. EDT

The Commander in Chief heard the buzzing, and saw the light on his phone in his dressing room. He pressed the speaker button. "Yes?"

"Excuse me, Mr. President, but you have a code red phone call on line three."

"Thank-you, Susie, put me through."

"Hello, Mr. President. This is Brigadier General Ralph Michaels from NASA. Sorry to bother you on a Sunday morning, but this is urgent."

"No problem, General, what is it?"

"Well, Sir, we have a problem with the Mars Expedition."

"What kind of problem?"

"I received a call from Mission Control, and they have lost communications with the manned space module on its way to Mars."

"What's happened to it?" The President said, alarm in his voice.

"At this point, we don't know. The mission has been flawless, until now. There has been no previous indication of something wrong. We are waiting to get pictures from the Hubble telescope, to see if the vehicle is still heading toward Mars. It was scheduled to enter into orbit around the planet in three days. We believe it should be kept top secret for now, until we learn more. I will notify you when I have more information."

"I'll be waiting for your call." He clicked off the phone.

Trying to sort the situation in his mind, Joe and Sally's face crossed his mind. They seemed so happy.

The First Lady's eyes bore into the sober face of her husband.

"What's the matter? Can you tell me?"

"Communications have been lost to the Mars Expedition. They're going to keep me informed. It's top secret for now."

"Do you still want to go to church?"

"I can't think of a better time to go, can you?"

CHAPTER 41
EVA

*Sunday, August 30, 2022, 11:13 a.m. Earth time EDT, En-
route to Mars*

Sally rubbed her head and felt a lump where her head bumped the wall as the module lurched.

"Are you all right? Joe asked, concerned.

"I think so. I have a small bruise on my head. But I don't think it's anything serious. How about you?

"I'm fine. Let's check the rest of the crew."

They floated through the portal to the eating area. There, the four other members of the expedition were busy analyzing the computer monitors. Sam, Joe's best man, moved around the cabin from one screen to the other checking all the systems that kept them alive. All indications were green.

Joe spoke first. "Is everyone all right in here? What do the readings say?" He floated over next to Sam.

"I think we are very lucky. None of us appear to be hurt and the systems are functioning. It appears we are going to live."

Joe gazed at his friend. He trusted his knowledge. They couldn't have a better crew member in this situation. Graduating summa cum laude from MIT and Princeton, Sam had Phd's in mechanical engineering, physics and civil engineering.

"We did suffer damage." The announcement came from Nelson, the Commander. "I sent a signal message twenty minutes ago to Houston and we haven't heard back yet. As you know, it takes nine minutes and thirty seconds to send a signal, and the same to get an answer back. I've not received one, yet. I'll give them another few minutes, but I'm afraid we've lost communications to and from Houston. All other systems are OK. I'm wondering if our radio antenna is functional."

Joe spoke up. "The antenna isn't visible from the portals. One of us will have to do an EVA, extravehicular activity, to check it. I'll volunteer."

Sally floated over to Joe. "I'll help you suit up. Do we have another antenna, if it's been knocked off?"

"No. But maybe it's bent."

****

Tom, second-in-command, opened the hatch to the airlock. Joe and Sally floated through. When Joe stood outfitted, Sally climbed back through into the module.

She moved quickly to the best window to see Joe leave the module. Tethered to the vessel, Joe disappeared around the side. I have nothing to do but wait.

Five minutes went by. Ten minutes went by. Finally, after fifteen minutes, the space walker pulled along the tether until he appeared in his waiting wife's view. Sally exhaled deeply. She knew how dangerous space walks could be.

When the pressure equalized in the airlock, Joe opened the hatch and climbed through to the cabin. He immediately floated over to his wife and gave her a hug.

"I'm back, he told her, and turned to Commander Nelson. "Our antenna is missing. We are on our own with no communications to or from Houston."

Nelson faced everyone. "Then we will follow procedures. Since everything else is functioning, we'll continue our mission. One of two things will happen. First, we'll stay on our plan and land. The habitat has its own radio system. If that works, and it should, we're back in business. Second, if that doesn't work, we'll wait until new equipment arrives from Earth. I'm sure the mission control people are tearing their hair out, wondering if we are still alive."

Sally spoke up, "Was there any indication as to what caused our antenna to be missing?"

"No. It could have been a number of things," answered Joe. "Most likely a micro-meteor hit us. Our spacecraft is made of the latest materials that are pretty good at deflecting objects that might hit us. There's a big dent in the side of the module, but the integrity is good and did not penetrate the skin. So we got off lucky this time. We can be thankful that it must have been small in size."

Nancy, the crew's physician, said, "Sally, let me take a look at your bruise and then I think the rest of us should get back to our duties. We have a lot to do if this mission is going to be a success."

Nelson answered, "You're right, Nancy, it's going to be difficult without the input of Houston, but we've trained for this scenario. We'll enter Mars' orbit in four days. We are fourteen days from landing on the surface. During our revolutions around the planet, we will take pictures and send out weather balloons as preliminary steps to our picking the best landing site near the North Pole. Then our landing sequence will begin. The target where our supplies are extends a mile in diameter. You all have been trained for this mission. An emergency team will be dispatched to us by Mission Control, but they won't reach us for about six or seven months. We're on our own. Let's get to work."

Joe turned to Sally. "You know; I think I have an idea."

"What's going on in that big brain of yours?"

"I think I can make an antenna and attach it to the space craft. I need to check our supplies and see if I have the articles to work with. I need to talk to Commander Nelson and Sam."

Sally followed Joe to where the Commander studied his computer indicators.

Joe tapped Nelson on the arm. "With your permission, I'd like to give it a whirl to fix the communication problem by building another antenna. The landing could be pretty hairy without communications from Mission Control in Houston, don't you think?"

"Hey, buddy, it's worth a try. Go for it. But what are you going to use for supplies?"

"I need copper wire, a pole, screws or something to connect the new antenna back to the original coaxial wire. I know if we can find the right items, I can make one. I have delved in ham radio operations, and I've made many antennas. It should work. It'll require another EVA, but I'd be glad to do it, again."

Nelson stared at the ceiling of the module with his hand under his chin. "You search in the extra compartments for what you need. I'll check the computer's manifest and see if extra copper wire is aboard. You'll have to look for a pole. We have screws."

Joe found a roll of wire. He stripped two support poles measuring eighty-inches apiece from three berths. Next, he cut them all in half and attached the poles together in the form of a T and wound the copper wire around and around the poles with Sally's help.

The finished antenna did not strike any of the crew as professional, but they all hoped it would be functional.

Joe emerged through the hatch along with the antenna and donned his EVA suit. Once the pressure was lowered and equal to the outside, he opened the outer door, and pulled the folded antenna through the opening. It barely fit. He carried more wire and a bag of tools attached to his side.

Sally manned her position at the portal nearest the antenna mount, and watched her husband float by holding onto the project design with one hand and the tether with the other until he disappeared around the side of the module.

Thirty minutes passed when the stress call came.

"Hey guys, I've got a problem." Joe's voice sounded rushed and labored.

"I tore my suit and am depressurizing. I'm trying to make it back to the hatch. I need some help. I'm already feeling the effects of hypoxia. It's getting harder to breath."

Sally waved her arms, flailing to get to the air lock faster. Sam copied Sally, trying to grab the air to pull him toward the hatch. They rushed through, and each one grabbed an EVA suit. Nancy followed, to help them dress into their suits. When they were ready, Nancy fled back through the entry and Sam pushed it shut. Precious seconds went by as they waited for the compartment to equalize to the outside. Finally, they opened the outside hatch and Sam connected a hook to the tether. Sally waited at the open hatch. Sam slid along it until, around the bend of the capsule, he spied Joe floating, unconscious—or worse. His best friend had pulled himself two-thirds of the way back to the entrance, but did not make it any farther. More seconds went by.

Sam gave one final grab of the line and reached Sam and immediately began pulling him to the life-giving orifice to the space capsule. Once there, Sally clutched hold of him, pulling him in as fast as she could. She had oxygen under pressure waiting. Sam pulled at the fasteners and slipped off Joe's helmet. Sally slammed the oxygen mask over his mouth. She could hear the rush of gas. They shut the latch to the outside, and waited until, the pressure allowed them to open the inner door. Nancy waited on the other side.

"I'll take over from here," the physician said.

Nelson and Tom pulled Joe's suit down to his waist, and held him down while Nancy started CPR.

Sally and Sam, space suits off, closed the inner hatch and rushed to Joe's side.

His lips were blue.

"Get the defibrillator," shouted Nancy.

"Here," said Tom.

Nancy yelled "CLEAR!" as she charged Joe's chest with one thousand volts.

Nancy used her stethoscope and announced, "His heart is beating. He's breathing."

Sally let out a deep breath, and her eyes welled. Thank you, Jesus.

His eyes fluttered open. He scanned everyone. His lips began to move. "What's going on? He mumbled.

Sally bent down and kissed him. "You almost died."

Confused, he said, "Oh, now I remember… the hammer poked my suit. Thanks, guys."

"We're glad you decided to come back to the world of the living," Sam teased, "although you didn't get the job done."

Joe frowned and turned his head toward Sam. "What do you mean, I didn't get the job done? Did you try to make a transmission?"

"No. But you tore your suit. You didn't finish the EVA."

Joe raised his eyebrows. "Has anyone tried to transmit? The antenna is up."

Tom rushed to the radios and called Houston. They waited precisely nineteen minutes and twenty seconds when a voice, sounding very excited, said, "This is Houston, Mars Expedition. We read you loud and clear. It's great to hear from you! Are you all right? What is your status?"

Commander Nelson replied, "We read you five by five, Houston. Our antenna broke off by an unknown cause. Joe did an EVA to fix it and it is presently working well. Joe ripped his space suit, on the EVA, but he's OK, thanks to Nancy. We will send you a full report. Everyone else is functioning at top levels. We are on schedule for landing on Mars in fourteen days, over."

Joe turned to Sally. "No one said it would be easy."

Sally smiled and glanced out the portal at the big red planet.

"We are both optimists. We need to be if we are going to survive our future on Mars."

CHAPTER 42
Mars Orbit

Wednesday, September 2, 2022, 10:09 a.m.,
Earth time EDT, Mars

Sam raised his head and gazed outside the Mars Expedition. The predominantly light orange planet loomed outside the portal. A curved horizon reminded him of his observations from the International Space Station orbiting Earth. Only instead of blues, greens and browns, slowly passing beneath him, this setting filled his vision with rusty, orange mountains and craters. Shades of brown, created by dust and sand, blown by vast windstorms, spotted the terrain. Coming into view on the horizon, the North Pole area displayed layers of white ice consisting of water and carbon dioxide. Their landing site lay here in the vast valley named Chasma Boreale. He turned to thoughts about his buddy, Joe, and Sally who would build their home and become the first humans to live indefinitely on Mars.

It had been a long journey. And still, two years remained on his mission before he and three other astronauts departed back to Earth. Others would come and go on subsequent expeditions, but as long as Joe and Sally remained healthy, they were the first true pioneers on Mars. He couldn't refrain from fearing for their safety. What dangers would they find? Would they survive?

He turned back to his duties to make a transmission.

"Houston, Mars Expedition, entering orbit on Mars at 1015 hundred hours. Everything is go, over."

CHAPTER 43
Life is Not Fair

Wednesday, December 2, 2022, 2:46 p.m.
EDT Earth time, Mars

"Are you sure, Sally? Did you check it twice?"

"Of course, Joe, I checked it three times! The tests are 99.9 percent accurate."

"Are you saying, we're going to have a baby? Wahoo! I have to tell the rest of the crew, immediately! Wait. How are you feeling? Are you sick or anything? Can I get you something?"

"Whoa. Whoa. Slow down. There will be plenty of time to pamper me in the next eight months. I am fine. I haven't been sick at all. Besides. I'm fit as I can be. There is no reason to change anything right now. I'll be able to keep my normal schedule, so please, don't treat me like an invalid, OK?"

"Agreed. I have to go break the news. This is history in the making."

Joe ran through Igloo II to find the rest of the crew members. Commander Nelson sat at the communication's desk entering data. The proud to-be-father couldn't help himself.

"Nelson. You are not going to believe this. Sally's pregnant."

"Oh, Joe, this is awesome news. I'll let the world know, right now, by radioing Houston. This is history in the making. We'll have to celebrate, tonight. There s a bottle of champagne, Dom Perignon 2002, I've been saving for a very special occasion, like a discovery or something. This is even better. Does anybody else know?"

"No, you're the first one I've seen. Where is everyone?"

"Tom and Nancy are sleeping. Their shifts begin in an hour. Sam is in the greenhouse watering the plants."

"I have to get to the greenhouse and tell my buddy Sam."

"Go ahead. I'll see you later. Congratulations."

Joe walked briskly through the pressurized passageway that led to the greenhouse. The systems he constructed purred, providing the correct atmosphere and light to grow the plants and vegetables. His salivary glands watered as he thought about eating fresh vegetables and ending the consumption of packaged meals brought with them. The corn stood two feet tall in their boxes making it difficult to find his friend.

"Sam?"

"Over here."

Rounding the fourth table, he spotted his buddy, watering the plants with melted polar ice scooped by the Rover the day before, and piled near the outpost.

"Sam, I have great news."

"I'm in the mood for good news after spending the entire morning gathering water ice and hauling it into the troughs."

"Sally is pregnant!"

Sam almost dropped his bucket. "Are you sure?"

"Yes. She is due next summer in eight months. Nancy will still be here, so she'll have a physician's care. We are making history."

"Congratulations, Joe. I'm happy for the both of you. But I'm a little nervous. We're a long way from a hospital."

"Oh Sam. Stop. She'll be fine. She hasn't even been sick or anything. She's as fit as a mother could be."

"I know. I'm sorry. It is great news. Has Nelson told Houston?"

"You bet. The news is all over the AP wires by now. We're already famous. This will change everything. Hopefully, in a good way."

"Are you going to stay and continue to live, here?"

"Of course. Sally and I have discussed it. Mars is our new home. We're pioneers."

"Aren't you afraid at all?" Sam asked his dear friend.

Joe pondered for a moment and answered, "Not really. There are dangers to living anywhere."

On his way back to the Igloo he thought, if I am honest, I do have fears. But how can I display them to anyone? We'll have to see what life deals out for my family.

CHAPTER 44
A Cry in the Night

Sunday, August 2, 2031, 3:08 a.m. EDT, Earth time, Mars

Sally nudged her husband, sleeping soundly next to her. "Joe, wake up. I think my water broke. The bed's wet."

"What? Your water...Is it time?" Joe's eyes were now wide open.

"Yes, I think so. Go wake Nancy."

Sally lay back down when the first squeezing grabbed at her abdomen. My first contraction. Oh, God, please let my baby be healthy.

****

Joe entered Nancy's quarters and shook her arm. "Nancy, wake up! Sally may be going into labor. She needs you."

Nancy was a light sleeper. "Sure thing. I'll get my doctor's kit, and be right there. Is that the wind I hear outside?"

"Yes," answered Joe. "We're getting a dust storm, as predicted by the satellite images. What a night for our baby to come into the world." He laughed, nervously. "I mean this world. Please don't be long. Her water broke."

"I'll be right there," replied the doctor as Joe exited back to Sally's side.

Sally had perspiration above her upper lip. "I'm glad you're back. I had a pretty strong pang just now."

"We need to start timing them."

"Oh, Lord! Here comes another one." She grabbed Joe's hand and he thought she broke his fingers, she clung so tight.

"Breathe. Breathe," soothed Joe. "The doctor's on her way."

Sally puffed in and out trying to cope with the contraction. Her face grimaced with pain.

Is this normal for the pain to be so bad so soon?

Sally screamed as Nancy entered the room.

Nancy palpated her abdomen.

"I'll take over." Send Nelson in here. He's manning his station in the radio room. Tell him I need help. You wait outside with the others.

Joe's eyes widened. "I want to stay here. I am supposed to help."

"No. I don't want two patients to take care of. You're white as a ghost."

Sally quieted down.

"OK. But if there's any trouble, you get me right away. Do you hear me?"

"Yes. Now get out of here."

Joe felt his heart race. Wasn't he supposed to help her breathe? They had practiced for weeks. Something must be wrong and Nancy wasn't telling him."

Joe stood outside his and Sally's room as he pierced through each of the crew with his eyes that begged for a consoler. Sam went to him and put his hand on his shoulder.

"You look awful. What's happening in there?"

"Sam, I don't know." Another scream came from the other side of the partition. "Has anybody here been through this?"

Tom spoke up. "Every childbirth is different, but my wife screamed like an Indian warrior, when she was in labor... maybe not quite as window shattering as Sally, but remember her lungs are very healthy. Sit down, Joe, this could take a while."

Joe followed Tom's suggestion and waited for Nancy to call him.

****

Nancy knew Nelson had been a medic in Afghanistan many years before he entered flight training. "Hand me that stethoscope, please, Nelson," the physician said. I'm having a hard time turning this little one. The baby is breech, and I can feel his bottom. He is a boy. I don't want to use forceps unless I have to. She continued to manipulate and knead Sally's abdomen trying to change the baby's position.

Finally, she gave up and said, "I have to do a Caesarian. There is no other choice." I have to get this baby out soon, or both Sally and the little one won't make it. The cord is visible and prolapsing.

"Hand me the Lidocaine. It is ready in that syringe to the right. Ya, that's it."

Nelson cleaned Sally's abdomen with Betadine solution.

After administering the sedative, Nancy explained to Sally what she needed to do.

Sally nodded, crying and groaning.

Nancy proceeded with a vertical incision while Nelson kept the bleeding to a minimum. Reaching into Sally's opening, the doctor pulled the slimy baby boy through the opening, and held the screaming newborn up to show his mother. Sally's sweaty face contorted to a smile. Nancy clamped and cut the cord. She handed the baby to Nelson who suctioned his mouth and cleaned him off. An injection of Ketamine was given to Sally. Nancy glanced at the clock and noted the time.

****

Another twenty minutes went by, while the doctor stitched Sally up. Finally, Joe was ushered in to meet his new son. Nelson handed the, now, sleeping baby to Sally, who laughed and cried at the same time. Joe rushed to Sally's side and kissed her. "We have a baby. There are now three of us."

Joe opened the baby's blanket to check him over. "A boy! We have a son. And he has all his fingers and toes. He is perfect!"

Sally motioned to Nancy who cleaned her utensils and said, "If it wasn't for our doctor over there, neither our son nor I would be here. Now, she has saved all three of us."

"You're quite a doctor, Nancy. Thank you."

Nancy grinned, while she washed her hands and arms. "You're welcome. Now, both of you get some rest."

Nelson, washed up and said, "I need to tell Earth the great news. If the new family will excuse me, I have to call Houston."

CHAPTER 45
Tragedy

Tuesday, August 2, 2035, 5:00 a.m. EDT, Earth time, Mars

"But I want to go. Please can I?"

"He could wear the space suit the astronaut, Lisa, used. She wore a small size," pleaded Sally.

"And it's my birthday! I'll be twelve. If I lived on Earth, I could hunt with a rifle," Jonathan argued.

Joe relented, "If we let you go, you must ride with me, and stay by my side at all times. We can only ride to the cliff. Then it's a long walk up a thousand-foot hill. We are taking extra air packs to last all day. Are you sure you want to go?"

"Yes. Yes. Oh thank you Mom and Dad. I'm growing up. I've only taken one trip to the Earth. The rest of my time has been spent here in the dome."

The next morning proved clear, with little wind, unusual for Mars. Joe and Sally, and Jonathan donned their suits and left the Igloo for the entrance to the dome.

Riding the four-man Rover, with a plow attached to the front, they drove toward the airlock.

Joe waved to a few neighbors, up at this early hour. He scanned the area. Corn stood ten feet in rows to his left. Crops, already harvested, resulted in empty furrows to his right. He felt proud of all that had been accomplished in the thirteen years they inhabited Mars. A variety of abodes and shops had been built since the Igloo II was constructed. A three-hundred-feet, in circumference, by fifty-feet tall dome, covered and protected them from the dangerous radiation emitted mainly by the Sun. Joe's suggestion to construct another dome inside the main one and fill the five-foot space between the two with water, successfully blocked ninety-nine percent of harmful solar particles. The dome shape allowed the howling winds to blow over them protecting the inhabitants from the frequent dust storms. And controlling the temperature of the water in this sheath, kept them a comfortable seventy-two degrees.

The outside painted a different picture. Although summer, without their special space gear, they would freeze or suffocate from the carbon dioxide atmosphere. But Sally and Joe were used to these unfriendly conditions. They survived many trips exploring for more water, and taking samples of various rocks to send back to Earth.

Joe enjoyed going on these searches. This time of year the carbon dioxide layer of ice melted, leaving beneath frozen water exposed. Today, they would venture to the ice cliff and try to find a way to the top to test the depths for more water. The water provided more than sustenance in liquid form. Machines isolated the oxygen for breathing and hydrogen for fuel.

Reaching the thousand-foot cliff took an hour on the rover. They followed the base, trying to find an opening that could be climbed to the top. After riding another hour, they reached a promising place.

"This is the location we've been searching for," Joe acknowledged. He scanned the slope that gradually made its way up as far as he could see.

"Time to hike, family." They stopped the Rover, and jumped out onto the sandy surface.

The three began climbing. After about five-hundred-feet the terrain steepened and their breathing became labored. Joe checked his timepiece. They had been moving upward fifteen minutes, stopping periodically to rest. The going proved to be rugged with boulders of ice to circumnavigate and small holes to step over. Joe began to wonder if they should have allowed Jonathan to come along.

"How are you doing, champ?" Joe asked his son.

"Fine. How are you doing, old man?" Jonathan said, laughing.

"I'll race you to the top," Joe challenged.

"You're on, silver edges!"

Off they went. Sally yelled as she laughed, "See you at the top." They had about three-hundred-feet to go.

At the summit, Joe joked, "I beat you."

"No you didn't. It was a tie."

Joe scanned the area. Ice stretched as far as they could see. He beckoned to his son. "Come help me take samples." After five minutes past, Joe turned to where they climbed the hill.

"Your mom ought to have been here by now. Go over to the edge and see where she is, Jon."

"Sure."

Jonathan peered down over the crest of the cliff and then returned to his father.

"She isn't here, yet."

"What do you mean? Did you see her?"

"No. She isn't anywhere."

Joe's stomach lurched. Sally always worked hard to stay in top condition. She should have had no trouble climbing the steep terrain and been at the peak by now.

He set down his pick, and ran over to where she should have crested over the top.

Jonathan told the truth. No Sally. Surely, she is behind a boulder sitting. Resting. But I don't believe it would take her this long.

He yelled to his son. "Get the pick and come on. We need to find your mother."

After calling her name and hearing nothing, Joe slid down the hill as fast as he could. When he had descended two-hundred-feet, he gasped.

In his path, a newly formed sinkhole encircled the area they traversed while climbing. He ran to the edge and peered down as far as he could see. He called her name, again. Nothing.

Joe used his flashlight, but the abyss descended down too far. Oh my god. Oh my god! Sally!

"We have to go get help," Joe yelled to Jonathan as he approached.

Jonathan's eyes widened. "That looks like a sink hole. Do you think Mom is down there?"

"Yes. Let's get going. We only have a few hours before she runs out of oxygen."

The twelve-year-old sniffed up tears. "Do you think she'll be all right?"

"I don't know, son."

Joe returned with other men. The distant sun had lowered considerably in the sky. They all began climbing the
eight-hundred-feet. Jonathan stayed home.

"I'm going down to get her," Joe said moving toward
the hole.

"No, Joe. You're too distraught. You'll only get killed
as well."

"We don't know if she is hurt. Besides, I'm the best
rope climber."

"No, Joe, let someone else go down. You have a son to
raise."

Bill, a recent arrival from Earth, tied the four-hundred-
foot rope, all they could find, around his waist, and descended into the hole. Slowly unwinding the curled rope, the remaining men held on to the end, keeping track of how much
they let out. At two hundred feet, Joe called the climber, "Do
you see her?"

"No, not so far."

They kept lowering the rope. The sun formed shadows
as it sunk toward the horizon. The rope kept uncurling until
the last man said, "we only have enough to hold on to the
end."

They all looked at Joe. One man added, "The sink hole
must go clear to the bottom. No one could survive that."

"But she had to survive. I can't live without her."

"Joe. I'm so sorry. We have to pull Bill up. He can't go
any lower. We have to get back to the dome or we're all going to perish. The rovers may not start if it gets too cold."

In shock, Joe stared at the hole. I don't believe it. We
were going to grow old together. She is the love of my life.
How will I tell Jonathan? There must be something we can
do. I can't leave her down there."

Bill finally made it to the top. It grew dark and colder.

One of the men wrapped his arm around Joe's shoulders. "Come on, Joe. You have Jonathan to think about now. If the winds start to blow, the dust will cover our helmet shields and the beacon, and we won't be able to find our way back to the dome. We'll all be lost forever out here."

Joe's arms hung down at his side. He felt numb, but descended down to the rover and headed back to the dome. His life was now meaningless. Sally meant everything.

When he arrived and entered the Igloo, Jonathan ran over to him. "Is she all right?"

"No, Jonathan, she fell too far down the sink hole. We had to leave her there…"

Jonathan grabbed his dad. Joe wrapped his arms around the wailing boy. They both sobbed.

Finally, Joe gazed into his son's eyes that reminded so much of Sally, and said, "It's you and me, now."

Jonathan nodded. Joe thought, I do have something to live for.

CHAPTER 46
Dr. Jonathan Cooper

Wednesday, September 30, 2050, 11:32 a.m.,
EDT, Earth time, Mars

The starship settled slowly into the airlock as a crowd of people stood on the inner tarmac waiting for the weekly arrival from Earth. Reaching normal pressurization and flushing of the carbon dioxide, the outer doors of the airlock closed, and the inner doors opened. The crowd, held back by an eight-foot fence, watched as the starship taxied toward them.

Jonathan waved to Joe as he deplaned. It wasn't difficult to pick his father out of the crowd. Although sixty-one, his dad stood taller than most of the other people greeting passengers.

Tired after the two-month and six-day voyage, at least it didn't take as long as his last trip of six-months. The Commander explained over the intercom, that a new ion engine powered the ship and shortened the expedition by five months.

Jonathan ran to his dad and hugged him. Ten years of communicating by computer proved to be a long time.

"Look at you. You're taller than I am," laughed Joe.

"You haven't aged at all, Dad," remarked the son. "You fair better in person."

"It's great to have you back, son."

"I must admit it's been a grueling ten years at med school, but here I am, graduated and ready to begin work."

"Come on. Let's go to Sal's Eatery. You're probably starved. We have a lot to catch up on. My Rover is parked over there."

Jonathan scanned the surroundings. "Boy, this place has grown. I wouldn't have known I landed on Mars if I hadn't have recognized the planet out the window and seen you. They built a bigger dome, didn't they?"

"Yes. The pavers on the roads eliminate all that dust we had to put up with, when you were a young boy. And they have been landscaping along the streets to make newcomers feel at home."

"How big is the place now?" Jonathan asked as he and his father climbed onto the Rover.

"The new dome covers ten-miles in diameter, with our old small dome close by. I'll take you for a ride later and show you around."

They arrived at the restaurant, and went inside.

A pretty middle-aged waitress walked up to them. "Hi, Joe. You want your regular table?"

"Sure, Beth. Do you remember my son, Jonathan? The last time you saw him, we were part of the original pioneer group, over ten years ago."

"Why, I don't believe it! You're as good looking as your dad."

"Thank you, ma'am, said the home comer.

"He just came from Earth, where he went to Princeton, Harvard Medical School, and MIT. He's a physician who specializes in robotics. We're going to all be machines one of these days. Doctors can replace almost every part of our bodies except our brains. That's where Jonathan comes in. He's trying to figure out a way to download our memories into a computer. Can you believe it?" Joe bragged.

"That's way over my head, Joe," Beth laughed. By the way, what are you two going to eat?"

She took down their orders and scurried away.

"I have news to tell you, Dad. As you know, Dan Alexander, that guy you always talked about? He's running for President. I like his platform a lot, and campaigned for him. Another thing. Have you been hearing the rumors that the Earth's orbit is supposed to cross an asteroid's debris path in a few years? I heard it at MIT. The Earth may collide with one or more of these asteroid pieces. They say a couple are over a half-mile in diameter."

"Yes, I've heard about both of those news items. I'm glad you're here with me, and not on Earth."

"Do you think it will really happen?"

"Who knows? Son, I have some news to tell you. It happened a year ago. Diggers were plowing water-snow by the ridge where we climbed and lost your mother sixteen-years ago. You know how we tried to find her then, but didn't? Well, they found her remains. We gave her a proper burial. I thought you would like to know that."

Jonathan's face turned to stone. He still grieved over the loss of his mother at twelve-years-old.

"I'm glad to hear that, Dad. She deserved it. Where is she buried?"

"Outside the dome in our official cemetery."

"Can we go there after lunch?"

"Of course."

"Dad. I have something else to tell you. I've met a girl. I think she is the one. She is also a doctor. In fact, we graduated together at Harvard. Her name is Rihanna. We kept in touch while I was at MIT, and she did her residency at a Boston Hospital. Dad, we're engaged. I didn't tell you about her because she didn't want to commit to a relationship until she graduated and did her residency. She reminds me of Mom. But she specialized in pathogenics and genetics. She's been offered a job on the Moon base, Correll.

'I'll also be moving to Correll. There's a new research lab there that I've been offered a position to be head of, and I've accepted. My love is Robotics, Dad, and the government has given us a fifty-million-dollar grant to develop a computerized brain. I want to download memories of a human cortex into a computer, and transplant the computer into the robot's brain. If I can do that, the computerized gray matter will make the robot an android. This is my goal. It's the future."

Joe studied his son. "I'm proud of you, Jonathan. You know that. I'll support you whatever you decide to do. The research sounds exciting. I am in the process of moving my enterprise from California to here on Mars. I've been working on a new EVA suit that is much easier to maneuver in, and enables a person to endure the elements, here, and on the other colonies. I am also thinking of getting involved in politics. How long are you staying on Mars?"

"I'll be staying seven Mar's days. And then I'm meeting Rihanna in Correll. We'll get married there. I'd like you to come to the ceremony. It will be sometime in January. Can you come?"

"Of course, Jonathan. I'm sure your Rihanna is a fine girl. I haven't been off Mars for twenty-eight years. It's time I visited another colony.

CHAPTER 47
Victory

Tuesday, November 3, 2050, 2:00 a.m. EST, Earth

Eddie clapped and waved his arms as he shouted to his boss, Dan Alexander.

"You won! The media declared you the winner two minutes ago!"

"Careful old man. You're going to have a heart attack."

Dan set down his sandwich on the kitchen table, and hurried into the living room to see for himself.

The video camera, set up beforehand, began whirring as he sat down and affixed his eyes to the 3D screen to witness history for himself.

"They announced you the winner, Mr. President," said Kristen laughing. We've won!"

"And what about you? You've become the First Lady elect."

The Alexander house filled with din. The friends and relatives in attendance stood up and began dancing and cheering. Everyone crowded around Dan shaking his hand, hugging him and slapping him on the back.

"I'm proud of you, Son, you did it," announced former Governor Alexander.

Dan turned to his father. "I guess it's a pretty good eighty-second birthday present, huh, Dad?"

"It sure is. I wish your mother were here to celebrate. She would have been as proud of you as I am. You're going to make a great President."

"Thanks, Dad."

Eddie jostled over to the President-elect and handed him the phone. "It's the White House," he whispered to his employer.

"I am taking this in the other room. I can barely hear with this commotion."

Dan rose and moved toward the den.

"Hello, Mr. President. How are you?" He closed the door behind him.

"The *quest*ion is, how are you? Congratulations. I'll be handing over the reins to you in a couple of months, and I'll be calling *YOU* Mr. President."

Dan raised his eyebrows. "That hasn't sunk in yet. It proved to be a close election until eleven o'clock when I pulled away."

"It's good to hear your voice, again," said the Commander-In-Chief. I haven't talked to you, in person, since I saw you in the Senate in October. My office will be arranging a meeting, soon. We have a lot to discuss. I'll let you get back to your celebrating. But first I must let you know, the Secret Service will be there before morning to protect you and your family. They'll replace the security you have now. Get some sleep. You'll need your rest."

Dan opened the den door while his dad announced, "It's been a long and exciting night, folks. I think we need to let Dan and Kristen get some sleep, don't you think?"

"What time is it?" asked Dan.

"Two fifteen. We need some sleep," Kristen agreed.

As the main campaign staff and close relatives bid their good nights, Dan and Kristen climbed the stairs to their bedroom, while Dan realized, tonight, their lives had changed forever.

CHAPTER 48
Security Briefing

Monday, January 18, 2051, 9:00 a.m., EST, Earth

Dan arrived at nine o'clock for his first daily security briefing being held at the White House. With two secret service men ushering him into the portico and the Cabinet-Briefing room, the Incumbent President welcomed him and asked him to sit down.

He expected a bigger room. The twenty-foot table and sixteen chairs took up most of the center. He didn't know how reporters could fit around the perimeter. In his mind he estimated there might be four feet from table to wall. But at the Daily Briefing, no media was allowed. Everyone was sworn to secrecy.

"Let's get started, shall we?" began the Commander-In-Chief. "First of all, let's welcome our next President."

They all clapped as Dan smiled and nodded.

"We wish you a successful and meaningful Presidency, in the coming dangerous times going forward. We have several topics to cover, today. Secretary of State Smith, please give us your report on the colonies."

"Yes, Mr. President. We now officially have ten colonies. For the record, they are listed as: the Moon, Mars, Mercury, Europa, Titan, three asteroids, Ceres, Vesta and Ida, and two self-supporting space stations named Elena and Adair. Three more colonies are being explored on asteroids 1999 RQ36, Lutetia, and Pallas. The ten colonies are setting up a joint Confederation and will be self-ruling within two years. An ambassador will represent each one in the United Nations, here on Earth.

"The Moon outpost, Correll, is successfully running a pathogenic and DNA laboratory, which is studying organic matter unfamiliar to Earth. Mining operations on Ceres has made a discovery of a new orange-colored metal called curbite. It is stronger than anything on Earth. It may have many uses in the future.

"The economies of the colonies are booming. Their gross national products have quadrupled every five Earth years. Commercial starships number more than three hundred, with the countries, United States, Russia, Britain, France and China leading in their construction. All the colonies are self-sustaining and growing. I have statistics on printouts that are being passed out as I speak.

"We do have a problem, however. Discord is occurring over the curbite issue. The asteroid, Ceres, mining the metal, feels entitled to all the profits. With this as a catalyst, many colonies are building a military system."

The Commander in Chief scowled. "Thank you Secretary Smith. Secretary of Defense, Adam Wellsley, what is your report on the asteroid, Seriod?"

"Well, Mr. President, most governments are taking part in our effort to deflect or destroy the ten break-up pieces of Seriod. We have had some success, and have destroyed five using nuclear means and lasers. Three were over a half of a mile in diameter. The impact date remains the year 2058. Proposals for actions are being generated by the most renowned scientists in the world. Other suggestions are kinetic impact, conventional rocket motor, and an ion beam motor. I have an explanation of all the proposals in the handout being distributed.

"In the event we can't avoid an impact with one or more of these celestial objects, we are preparing an underground bunker to accommodate key members of government and their families, including all the people in this room, in a salt mine located in the Mid-West. You will receive plenty of notice if it becomes necessary. Other key people such as scientists, leaders of foreign powers, and medical personnel, will be accommodated in other locations throughout the world. We hope to maintain satellite communications after such an Impact Event."

"Thank you, Mister Secretary. Mr. Shellsberger, I believe you have a report on an economic development for Earth?"

"Yes, Mr. President. The new world currency is scheduled for production in Philadelphia, beginning April twentieth of this year. It will be similar to the European Euro, but will have worldwide distribution. I will have more information at the next meeting."

"OK. Scientist, Roger Miller, you have an announcement on two developments in the medical field?"

"Yes. As you know, the Space Program has provided many innovations to increase our longevity and chance of survival on Earth and in space. My laboratory has developed, through genetics and DNA modification, means to expect a human to live at least one-hundred and fifty years or more. We are also proceeding in the Moon laboratory, at Correll, with development of a computer program that will have the capacity to download a person's memories from his or her brain into a computer and from that point, be able to record all further cranial activity and total function, and appear to be the former human. The young doctor and brilliant scientist, Jonathan Cooper, son of the famous Senator Joe Cooper of the Solar Confederation, is leading the research. If he succeeds, we will have our first Android, and will enable robots to live in all conditions, indefinitely. There are many issues to be addressed with these developments, such as religious objections and ethical procedures. No public announcement will be made until these issues are addressed."

The cabinet members exchanged wide-eyed glances.

"Thank you, Doctor Miller. We look forward to your future reports. If there are no *Quest*ions, this concludes our Daily Briefing. Thank you all for coming." He turned to the President-elect. "Dan, how would you like to see the Oval Office?"

Dan stood, realizing this confidential briefing foreshadowed the new world he had entered into. Many of the Cabinet members came over and shook his hand and wished him well.

The President rounded the twenty-foot briefing table and said, "This way. You need to learn your way around. I'll show you your office where I spend an average of sixteen hours a day. It's customary for you to redecorate the room. You can talk to Kristen about that. I imagine she will be making many changes."

Dan smiled, and felt butterflies in his stomach. He couldn't believe he walked in the most famous of all houses.

After a tour of the Oval Office, the President bid him farewell.

"I have to get back to work. The world doesn't give me much time to relax. But I've enjoyed our meeting, again,

Dan, and we'll converse in two days at the inauguration and ball on the 20th. You'll be swamped after that. Spending two terms in this office, it'll be nice to get a break. I may go back into law practice. Or I may go fishing. Who knows?"

The leader and the President-elect shook hands. Dan's secret service men summoned, he completed another brief tour, and exited the White House to ride to his Washington apartment in Georgetown. In two days he wouldn't be able to leave the big house with so little fan-fare. Every move he made would be planned. Privacy gone. Walks in the park or the Smithsonian, gone. But he couldn't help being awed and excited. He anticipated the challenge. His new world had begun.

CHAPTER 49
Life On Correll

Tuesday, June 15, 2051, 8:00 a.m., EDT Earth-time, Mars

"I appreciate you walking me to the lab, Jon."

"No problem."

The engaged Jonathan and Rihanna paced down Duvall Street and turned left at the corner. In front of them stood Sterling Laboratories reaching up until the structure seemed to touch the base layer of the four-hundred-foot dome covering Correll. The building glowed silver in color and reflected the morning sun lighting up the transparent ceiling of the lunar city. Workers, like them, walked through the doors of their new workplace one by one passing through security as they entered.

Once inside, Jonathan stopped and turned to Rihanna. "You have a great day. Don't let any of those micro-bugs eat you."

"Don't worry. I'm packing a micro gun."

They both laughed and turned to go opposite directions to their jobs. Rihanna disappeared on the East elevator to the Pathogenics Department, while he pressed the button to take the elevator to the West. On the fourth floor he entered the Department of Bionic Robotics.

"Good morning, Director," spoke a robot.

"How are you doing, today, Robert?" replied Jonathan. "Are you scheduled to go outside the dome, again, later?"

"Oh, Doctor Cooper, it was awful. So cold I had to turn my sensors off. Please don't send me out there to freeze."

"OK. We'll keep you inside. We wanted to test the cold on your switches. You passed with flying colors."

"Thank you so much, Director."

"Robert. How about getting me a cup of coffee? Two creams."

The Robot went scurrying down the corridor. Jonathan smiled. My best achievement.

He passed into his laboratory, turned on the computers and studied the indications. All systems appeared to be functioning properly. After putting on his white lab coat, he entered his office and sat down at his desk to read the lab reports from assistants, turned in at the end of yesterday. The four employees would not be arriving for another half hour.

"Here's your coffee, Doctor Cooper." Robert set the steaming cup down on his boss's desk.

"How did the night go, Robert? Did you catch any burglars?"

"Of course not, Director. You know this place is more secure than anywhere else in Correll."

"Just checking. I want you to earn your keep, you know."

Jonathan studied his creation. Robert earned him the Lemelson-MIT Award as a senior, for perfecting the android.

The robot had self-aware intelligence displaying many emotions. With an IQ of 140, Robert performed tasks, learned equations, and explained quantum theory when asked. He energized with the installation of a fusion-based power cell. Unlike the creations of early present century, Robert resembled a thirty-year old man, standing six-foot-three, with brown hair and brown eyes.

Jonathan's purpose for sculpting his android in this fashion served to represent an average human being. Duplicates were being generated at a factory on the other side of Correll. Production could not keep up with demand, and the factory in the next year would need its own dome to accommodate the increase in production. Jonathan foresaw the expansion, and bought a twenty-percent stake in the company with trust money from his father. Hopefully, he and Rihanna would never lack for an income in the future.

But he was not satisfied. His aspirations lie in downloading his personal memories into the computerized brain of his likeness. The fifty-million dollars presented by the United Nations World Government, would enable him to accomplish this task. The implications were enormous, and security was tight. Sterling Laboratories monitored his whereabouts with an implanted cell, to protect him in the event he became a kidnap victim. The location on the Moon base insured some security. But times were changing and his safety proved paramount.

Jonathan did not *Quest*ion the integrity of the company. He knew the CEO and most of the Board of Directors. He trusted that his company would use the Androids for the indefinite survival of mankind. It was their motivation. Androids could endure harsh conditions anywhere in the Solar System and beyond. All of the colonies' inhabitants needed a special EVA suit, designed by his dad, to venture away from the domes being built. The fear existed the domes could lose their integrity and fail, exterminating masses of human colonists. With military buildups occurring the need accelerated.

"Good morning, Director. Good morning, Robert," sang Lenora as she breezed into the lab.

"What are you so happy about?" *Quest*ioned Jonathan.

"I'll have you know I received my doctorate papers online. I'm so excited. How about a raise for your senior assistant?"

"Not a chance. You already make almost as much as I do."

"Well, it was worth a shot. Robert, would you get me some coffee? Black. Thanks, you handsome devil."

"Of course, Miss Lenora," said the obedient android. He scurried off down the hall.

"What time is your and Rihanna's wedding next Saturday? Was it one or two o'clock? I still need to get you two a present."

"Two o'clock. It's only going to be a few people and Robert."

"I like small weddings. Too bad you are so engrossed with your work that you can't take a honeymoon."

"We'll take one next year if my project is completed."

"Where will you go?"

"Lenora please get to work. The others are already working.

"What kind of a boss are you?"

Jonathan scowled.

"All right. All right. I'm heading to my computer. You're no fun."

The director watched her hurry to her desk. He wasn't upset with her. He couldn't be. Once she started, she proved her worth. And now she had her PHD in Robotics. Her pro-

duction and ideas excelled. He didn't really have any com-
plaints.

She turned her head and looked at him from her desk.

He smiled at her, briefly, as Robert handed her coffee,
and returned to his project.

CHAPTER 50
Another Wedding

Saturday, June 19, 2058, 1:49 EDT Earth time

"You look well, as usual, Dad. Thanks for coming all the way here from Mars to my wedding. There will be eight witnesses including you. I hope you don't mind no hoopla. Rihanna and I wanted it to be simple. Besides, we don't know many people in Correll."

"No problem, Jonathan. I wouldn't miss my son's wedding. Hey. You'd better get up to the altar. The judge is waiting for you."

"OK. Talk to you after the ceremony. I love you."

"Love you, too."

Jonathan hurried to the front of the Court House room while music began to play from a portable computer Rihanna's mom brought for the occasion. Soft and appropriate for slow dancing, the music cued heads to turn to the back of the small court room. There, dressed in a white, just below the knee creation, Rihanna began slowly marching to the front of the court room to meet her soon-to-be husband. Simple, but elegant, her mother had picked out the lace over taffeta dress, by a well-known designer on Earth, in New York. With a few alterations, it fit Rihanna perfectly over her slim five-foot-eleven figure. She chose to wear her waist-length blond hair up in curls on top of her head. She did not wear a veil.

When Jonathan saw her, their eyes locked. His welled, as he watched her come toward him. She was the girl of his dreams, and soon she would be joined with him in matrimony. He thought back to their meeting in a biology class at Harvard. She stood out from all the other women. Her beauty drew him to her, and although shy from the lack of social graces growing up on Mars, he started a conversation. They had similar interests in science and medicine and soon everyone knew they were a couple. They shared an apartment with two other students while he commuted to MIT and she finished her PhD in Pathogenics at Harvard.

Now, she stood next to him, and the judge's words seemed far away. He repeated his vows, and in five minutes, when he put the ring worn by his mother on Rihanna's finger, the judge pronounced them man and wife. He kissed her soundly, and smiled.

Congratulations resounded from all in attendance, and they all met out on the steps of the courthouse.

"Let's go celebrate," said Joe as he put his arms around the bride and groom's shoulders.

Rihanna and her mother had made reservations at Harper's Restaurant for a quiet reception. They now entered their respective rental vehicles, and drove down two blocks, to the eatery.

"Congratulations, Mrs. Cooper, whispered Jonathan into his bride's ear."

"I love you," responded Rihanna, smiling.

They kissed.

Jonathan couldn't remember when he had been happier.

CHAPTER 51
Address to Nation

Wednesday, March 15, 2058 8:55 p.m., Earth

"Are you ready, Mr. President?" asked the Chief of Staff.

"Yes. Where is my speech?"

"It's on the teleprompters, Sir, and on a monitor on the podium."

The President entered the East Room and stopped behind the podium. He waited for the cue on the television camera to light.

The cameraman raised his arm to the side and someone counted down to one. The cameraman pointed to President Alexander. The clock clicked, 9:00 p.m. The light went on:

"Good evening, my fellow Americans. I come to you, tonight, with grave news and a heavy heart.

As you know, several years ago the asteroid, Seriod, collided with a comet and exploded. The debris formed clouds of smaller pieces that scattered through our solar system. One cloud will pass through the orbital path of Earth.

The governments of the world have tried many methods to destroy or deflect these near Earth objects, or NEOs. We have used nuclear weapons, kinetic impacts, ion beams, focused solar energy, conventional rocket motors and other proposals offered by the best scientists on the Earth.

Some NEOs were blown up. Others deflected. However, one, a half-mile wide, heads toward a direct impact with Earth and will enter our atmosphere on June 11, 2058, three months from now. Scientists have determined the site will be Morocco, on the Northwest coast of Africa. People will be evacuated in that area. However, affects will be felt throughout the world.

We are initiating a plan for the citizens of the United States. At the bottom of your screens, you see a web site address to enter into your computers and phones. On this web page are instructions for you to begin preparing for this Impact Event. For those few without computers, information will be available at your local government offices.

Supplies to build shelters and fortify existing structures, along with food staples, will be distributed at local stores within two weeks.

Rest assured. Your government is taking steps to insure the United States' survival. If we work together, we can deal with this crisis, and remain the best country on Earth.

Good night, God bless you, and God bless America.

President Alexander took the White House elevator up to his living quarters.

"How did it go?" Kristen said hurrying over to Dan as he walked slowly into the living room.

"My leg hurts."

"What? Which one?"

"My new bionic leg. Although it has feeling now, it is a curse. Sometimes I wish I had my old plastic prosthesis back. Whenever I'm under a lot of stress it hurts. And it aches most of the time. I need a button to disable it."

"Someday they'll invent one. In the meantime, come over to the couch and lay down for a while. I'll massage your leg. Maybe, you shouldn't have run for a second term."

"I'll be fine. Besides, I've grown fond of this house."

He reclined on the couch. "I need to talk to you, anyway."

Kristen sat down on the sofa next to Dan and began kneading his aching leg.

"That feels good. I appreciate it. Are we alone?"

"Yes. Elsie has gone home for the night. She leaves at seven when supper is finished. What did you want to talk to me about?"

Dan scowled and said, "We need to begin packing our essentials. The military will be moving them to an underground bunker in Kansas. It's classified exactly where we are going. A runway, with all the electronic navaids installed to allow the aircraft to land in all weather conditions, has been built for our new Airforce 1. The plane is now equipped with fusion-energized engines and will shorten the trip from Washington to our destination to twenty minutes once airborne. We will leave June 9th at five p.m. The salt mine will be our home until it is safe to surface again. All governmental operations will be conducted from these caverns. I'm told the temperature in the mine is fifty-six degrees year around. However, a generator will keep us comfortable in our quarters."

"The general public will build shelters above and below ground or fortify existing structures. We are hoping out of four-hundred-million people in the US, sixty million will survive."

"Only sixty-million?"

"We'll be lucky if that many survive the fire storms, tsunamis, earthquakes and the cold that will come from the dust clouds."

"What about our family members?"

"The bunker will accommodate six-hundred people. Between the two of us, we can select forty friends and relatives. The caves are extensive. That's why they were selected. Honey, please stop crying."

"I can't help it. So many people are going to die like the dinosaurs."

"We hope to save as many as possible."

"How long will we be underground?"

"We will test the surface each month until it's habitable."

"Oh God, please help us."

CHAPTER 52
Impact!

Sunday, June 11, 2058, 8:06 p.m., Corelle, the Moon

"Honey, would you check on Rune? It sounds like he's crying in his room."

Rihanna turned away from the telescreen on the wall. "I'll bring him out here. I don't want to miss the moment of impact. I am so thankful my mother, father and brothers made it off Earth before this horrible event happens. The Seriod meteor must be getting close." She hurried to their three-year-old's room.

Moments later she returned, carrying the sleepy youngster. "He's still afraid of the dark. His night light must have burned out." She sat down on the chair and rocked the boy while she and Jonathan, once again, became glued to the 3-D monitor.

In the lower, right-hand corner of the screen the digital countdown sent chills down Jonathan's spine. Six minutes, thirty-two seconds. Thirty-one. Thirty.

It was history in the making. The Earth loomed in the background, a blue, white and green sphere. Serene. Majestic.

But in moments, a chaotic impact would make the waters around the event boil, and the land incinerate and vaporize, forming a crater visible to Jonathan and Rihanna on the Moon. They were safe. But not so for billions of people around the Earth. Hunkered down in their fortified basements or caves, millions prayed they would not be swallowed by a tsunami, earthquake, or consumed by fire.

The countdown continued. Satellites projected images of the fireball entering the Earth's atmosphere. Half the monitor displayed the Earth, half the fragment of Seriod hurling toward the surface in the vicinity of Northwest Africa.

Jonathan's stomach churned. Rihanna stared. Rune slept. One minute, ten seconds. Then, fifty-nine, fifty-eight, fifty-seven...

The one-mile in diameter meteor entered the Earth's atmosphere. An explosion of light lit up the Moon's night sky as the projectile penetrated the magnetosphere. Three, two, one...

IMPACT!

Jonathan's mouth dropped open. Rihanna's cheeks were wet.

As the celestial fragment met its target, the collision within seconds compressed the air creating a fireball, turning night into day. Like a stone dropped into water, the one-mile in diameter impactor splashed debris thousands of feet into the air, vaporizing ground zero. A shockwave, birthed by the impact, flattened surrounding structures and trees, and spread outward for a hundred miles. The resulting twenty-two-mile cavity at the impact sight could not be seen due to the fireball and dust cloud rising miles into the night sky over Morocco.

Jonathan thought about the repercussions after this Earth shattering event: Earthquakes shaking the world's faults while acid rain drenched the planet, killing much of the flora. The ozone layer becoming depleted letting in deadly solar radiation to the atmosphere. Temperature changes occurring and lasting weeks. People he knew and loved not surviving.

It will be days before I know the massive death tolls. As shocked as I am, it is a repeat of celestial bodies colliding. Nothing new. My home, the Moon, is covered with pocks formed by such strikes. But not in the last hundreds of years.

Life on Earth changed in an instant. The birth planet of the human race might now require superficial domed cities, like the colonies in the solar system. It could take millenniums for Earth to recover. Technologies developed by the expansion of the Space Program could save millions of people.

"I don't know if I can sleep, but we probably should go to bed. I'll carry Rune to his room."

Jonathan picked the sleeping boy up from Rihanna's arms as they made their way to their sleeping quarters.

"We must enjoy each day as it comes," whispered Rihanna in bed.

"Yes. Who knows what tomorrow might bring?"

CHAPTER 53
The New Land

Wednesday, May 16, 2059, 8:15 a.m., Earth

"Are your bags packed, Kristen? It's time to leave this cavern and see what it is like up on top."

"Yes, honey, I'm ready," said the President's wife.

Although his stomach churned, President Dan Alexander knew it was time to surface from the shelter six-hundred feet below ground. Anxious at what he would see, the survivors needed his visible leadership back in the White House in Washington.

A secret serviceman approached him. "Right this way Mr. President."

Kristen and Dan ducked their heads and entered one of dozens of vehicles used underground for the last few months to transport them to various areas of the cavern. This time, it led them to the main elevator where they would make the ascent to the surface.

Dan's ears popped as his entourage rose to a new world.

Finally, they reached the top, and the elevator doors opened to the reception room. They all were given masks to protect them from the residual dust swirling in the air they would encounter outside. The twenty people followed the President and Kristen to a fifty-foot by thirty -foot steel-covered entrance. At the push of a button by a guard, the heavy chains began to grind as it lifted the massive door and exposed them to the elements.

Breathing through the Cooper Industries' masks, as a precaution, everyone stepped outside into the elements. Although May in the Midwest United States, Dan thought the temperature must be below freezing since frost covered the tarmac leading to Air force one. And his hands were cold. His watch read 9:35 a.m., but the sky appeared like dusk as the blood red Sun rose in the East. The only sounds to be heard came from the blowing heated air of the auxiliary power unit of the big jet. The trees, naked without leaves, stood barren. Tiny shoots of green grass rose up out of the ground giving hope to the brown landscape. The air smelled musty through his mask. He could hear the words "eerie" and "unearth-like" from his entourage, walking behind him. He did not hear or see any fauna. Had any survived?

The flight took twenty minutes during which he received briefings from the members of his cabinet and generals who accompanied him. Kristen spent the time staring out the window at the orange haze and brown landscape stretching endlessly. They landed at Andrews Air Force Base where the Commander-In-Chief boarded one of three Marine helicopters that whisked all of them toward the White House south lawn. Dan observed a few cars and trucks on the highways. Mostly military.

A state of emergency dictated government mandates and orders. Two months earlier, the mass project to get the country back operating again included announcements to the population, by troops. They went from house to house spreading the news to exit their safe havens and report to government stations within their area. Census recruits compiled information to direct people to jobs necessary to reestablish the infrastructure within their communities. Slowly, electrical power and other services became available, and in an organized manner, the government began to function, distributing goods, such as food and gasoline.

The country woke up after its year's hibernation. As they flew over the city, he noticed commercial trucks making deliveries. Good, he thought. People must be receiving the word it was safe to exit their bunkers and basements.

Luckily, the United States escaped most of the damage caused by the impact. Although a global orange cloud hung over the country, and the temperatures remained cold, the country was determined in March to be habitable. Farmers planted crops of corn and wheat in the Southern states. Enough sunlight seeped through the haze to enable the grains to grow, insuring a food supply. In the meantime, storages of food held out.

****

"It's great to see you again, Susan," President Alexander said to his favorite staff member as he walked through the door. "The house looks the same. It sure is good to be back."

"Yes, Mr. President, we have much to talk about."

Dan peered into her eyes. "Are you O.K.?"

"Oh yes. I mean so much has happened. But I'm fine. The accommodations were as good as could be expected. I arrived back here two weeks ago."

"I'm glad." He smiled at her one last time, then turned to his guests, and said, "Right this way, gentlemen. Our work, in Washington, has once again begun."

CHAPTER 54
Ceres

Tuesday, August 6, 2060, 1015 a.m., Asteroid Ceres

Jonathan peered out the two-feet square window of the starship as it turned to make its approach to the planet-shaped asteroid, Ceres. As the vehicle slowed to descend vertically into the dome's center, he observed the mining facility. Tall drilling rigs stretched as far as he could see. Each appeared to be at least three-hundred feet in the air, almost reaching the top of the dome. Mounds of curbite rising one-hundred feet or more, were piled near the rigs. Bull-dozers loaded the metal onto moving belts transporting the precious commodity to stations in the distance. Robots operated the machinery. Offices lined the tarmac where businessmen from other colonies dealt for the valuable metal.

Jonathan came to Ceres to buy several containers of curbite to be shipped to his laboratories. Scientists discovered ways to mix curbite with other common metals and make the strongest and most versatile commodity known to exist in the Solar System. curbite could be used to fortify starships and prevent radiation from harming its human occupants. Domes, such as the one on Ceres, were made with curbite mixed with silicon to prevent the hostile environment from penetrating and harming the occupants.

But Jonathan had a new purpose for wanting the orange metal. He would construct his Androids with it, making them strong and durable enough to exist, indefinitely, under most conditions.

As he walked down the tarmac passing armed guards, a man approached him holding out his hand and asked, "Are you Jonathan Cooper from Cooper Industries?"

"Yes, I am. Are you Devin Leander?"

"Yes. Good to meet you, Doctor Cooper. Please come inside."

More guards in uniforms with "Security Personnel" stamped on the sleeves stood in front of the doors and moved aside when Jonathan and Mr. Leander approached.

Once inside, Jonathan asked, "Why are there so many armed personnel?"

"To protect us from any would be attackers trying to take over the base," answered the businessman as he sat down behind a grey metal desk.

Jonathan sat down in front of him. "Has there been trouble?"

"Not yet. But there are rumors and stories of unrest. curbite is becoming more valuable than gold. The colonies are starting to bicker over prices and who should control it."

"Who does control the prices?"

"Right now the government of Ceres. But we're accused of not being fair. Have you heard about the pirates?"

"No. What pirates?"

"The ones who are attacking our transports taking curbite to the colony of Europa. There is where the new starships are being built. curbite is being used to fortify their fuselages. It's said that they will be the next generation of starcraft."

"Pretty soon it will only take a day to get around the Solar System."

The man laughed. "You're probably right. As his smile faded he asked, "So. How much of this curbite do you need?"

"Three of your three-foot-square boxes. How long before I get them?"

"I can have it ready, today." Mr. Leander rubbed his nose. "Say. What are you going to use it for? Building a spaceship?"

Jonathan scowled at this intrusive man. "No. I'm conducting a government project that I am not at liberty to discuss."

The man raised his eyebrows and returned to the business at hand. "If you will give me your money transfer card, I will submit your order."

Jonathan worked his hand into one of his pockets.

A sudden deafening explosion sent him and Mr. Leander to the ground. Sirens began to blare.

Alarmed, Jonathan picked himself up and ran to the window. Several starcraft could be seen through the clear dome whizzing past as laser beams tried to bore holes into the shield built to withstand such an assault.

Mr. Leander yelled, "We're being attacked! Follow me."

Jonathan ran, following the salesman to a door at the rear of the building. They entered a small room, about ten-

feet square. A light illuminated as the door clunked shut behind them.

"This is my shelter," said the breathless, Mr. Leander.
"We'll be safe in here. This is the third time this month
we've been attacked."

Jonathan shivered. "I thought you said there hadn't been
any trouble, yet. Are you sure? That was a big bang out
there. Who would attack us?"

"Probably, Xanadu, the Titan Colony. It has become in-
creasingly hostile, lately. The bomb you heard sounded like
one of theirs. They are trying to blow a hole in the secured
entry. So far, they haven't succeeded."

"I wish I would have known of the danger. I wouldn't
have made a trip here."

"Too late, now," the Ceres businessman answered,
frowning.

"Is this place armed?" asked Jonathan.

"Yes. We recently installed a new dome fortified with
curbite. It will protect us from the missiles thrust at us. We
also have a fleet of starcraft with laser guns. They're being
used as we speak. We are planning to construct an arsenal.
With these attacks, I'm sure it will be soon."

Another siren wailed. "What's that?" Jonathan shouted.

"We're in the clear. It's safe to go out now."

Mr. Leander led the way back out to the main office.
They both moved to the window and gazed outside. The in-
truders were gone. Robots worked as though nothing had
happened. The warcraft, one by one, re-entered through the
orifice and settled down onto the tarmac. Jonathan counted
six of them. Nothing appeared to be damaged. Curbite had
done its job protecting the inhabitants.

"I'm amazed," exclaimed Jonathan. "I thought we were
dead."

"Curbite is remarkable stuff," the salesman said. "It's worth stealing. And we're the only place where it's been found so far."

Jonathan paid the man and headed toward the door, anxious to leave this place. In all his years he had not known politically troubled times. Since Earth's asteroids, the colonies had worked together for the common good. But it appeared that times were changing, and all because of an orange metal named curbite. In the end, would curbite cause the survival of mankind? Or the death of peace?

CHAPTER 55
Attack on Europa

Saturday, December 7, 2060, 9:27 a.m., Correll, Moon

"Jonathan! Come look at this!" shouted Rihanna to her husband who fixed Rune his breakfast in the kitchen. "Come and see what's happening on Europa."

Jonathan told his five-year-old son to eat his cereal, and rushed to the living room to see why his wife sounded so urgent. Rihanna pointed to the five-foot-wide screen on the wall.

"What's happening?" he said as he turned up the sound on the remote.

"Somebody is attacking Europa! The reporters are saying it's an act of war. Why would anyone bomb Europa? It's a peaceful manufacturing settlement," quizzed distraught Rihanna. She wrung her hands and stared at the images of the warcraft bombarding the dome where new starcraft were being constructed.

Satellite pictures played out the assault on live pro-gramming. If the dome became compromised, the people inside would die. Visions of several Titan fighters swept toward the dome as lasers shot out red beams of light hitting the life-rendering shroud cutting into it like butter.

Rihanna shrieked when she saw the gaping hole in the side of the dome. All the pressurized and climate controlling gases gushed out of the orifice.

"They are killing everyone!" she sobbed and finally covered her eyes and wept as she collapsed onto the sofa. Never in their lives had they experienced such aggression by other members of their own species. Horrid as it was to see the asteroid hit the Earth, this was a man-made terrorist act.

Stone-faced, Jonathan sat down next to his wife putting his arms around her, trying to comfort her.

Rune ran into the room, with fear-filled eyes and jumped onto the couch. "What is it, Daddy?" the young boy uttered with wide green eyes.

"It's all right, Rune. Come here and sit on my lap, son."

Rune snuggled down on his father's lap, while Jonathan encircled one arm around Rihanna and one around Rune. He knew life as they knew it had just changed. And he knew why…these ruthless invaders wanted the curbite. Would they get it?

CHAPTER 56
War Declared

Monday, December 9, 2060, 9:00 a.m.
Colonial Solar Confederation Headquarters, Mars

The light at each representative's seat-station lit, indicating the commencing of the emergency assembly of the Colonial Solar Confederation. Seventy-one-year-old Joe Cooper extinguished the illumination and turned his attention to the speaker standing at the podium in the center of the round, two-thousand capacity legislative chamber. Built to conduct the business and legislative matters of the thirteen colonies, today, they met to discuss civil war.

Joe adjusted his earpiece that would translate into English the words spoken by the Chinese speaker at the podium. In politics for the last ten years, he, along with nineteen others, represented the Mars colony. He enjoyed being in the middle of the decisions made that affected the affairs of Mars, his beloved home for thirty-eight years. He had seen the Mars colony change from a few "igloos," to a thriving metropolis.

But today, his stomach churned. Xanadu, the Titan colony, had turned rogue, killing thousands and stealing curbite stockpiled on Europa, one of Jupiter's peaceful moons. The league of colonies could not tolerate Xanadu's aggression any longer. Danger abounded. Rumors of war permeated the news media. As much as Joe hated the thoughts of war, the inhabitants of Saturn's largest moon must be stopped.

The Chairman spoke.

"We are gathered here, today, to vote on an issue we hoped would never arise in our young confederation—an act of war. Since the Colonial Solar Confederation's conception seven years ago, we have co-dependently and successfully worked to establish a ruling body that has overseen the establishment of a productive and life-insuring group of colonies. Until now.

"With Earth recovering from its own tragedy, the twelve colonies represented, today, must deal with the rogue colony, Xanadu, on our own. The terrorist acts must be punished.

"Our reconnaissance missions have revealed a massive military build-up on Titan. It must be stopped and reversed. A Declaration of War has been delivered to each representative. I trust each one of you has studied the contents. With the appropriate motion, we will vote on these actions, which will take effect immediately. We are open to discussion at this time"'

Deliberations began.

Joe listened with a heavy heart. When would violence give way to peaceful resolutions to grievances held by opposing factions? Technology outpaced human evolution. The destruction and annihilation of mankind hung in the balance.

I had hoped that humans had transitioned into a new era of peace and prosperity.

Once again, a light illuminated on his screen. It was time for a vote.

With a reluctant finger he pushed the affirmative button to declare war on Xanadu.

The vote proved unanimous.

Sadly, the assembly dismissed. He rose and headed toward the door. It opened to familiar surroundings, but had changed forever.

Joe knew this historical event meant changes for him and his family. How would this affect traveling to see Jonathan? What dangers lay ahead?

CHAPTER 57
President Alexander is Sought for Help

Monday, December 9, 2060, 10:00 a.m., Earth

Dan held the curtain aside and stared across the White House lawn. War. How could the Solar Confederation be at war? What was wrong with Xanadu? Didn't they realize what they had done?

The President's thoughts diverted to the phone ringing. He turned and sat down at the desk in his oval office.

"Yes, Melinda?"

"Mr. President, the Ambassador of the Colonial Confederation has arrived. Should I send him in?"

"Sure. I'm ready."

The entrance to the President's office opened and the Ambassador, flanked by two men and two women carrying notepads and recorders, entered the room. Two of the President's aides followed behind.

Dan stood and walked toward the group, holding out his hand to welcome the Ambassador.

"We meet again, Mr. Ambassador. I'm sorry to have to meet under these developments, but it is good to see you." He extended his arm toward the center of the room where two couches faced each other, and added, "Come sit over here where you will be comfortable. Can I offer you something to drink?"

The portly middle-aged man, along with his entourage, moved to the sitting area. The Ambassador sat down on the blue sofa while the other three sat on surrounding chairs. The President sat opposite him. The aides stood with electronic notepads behind the couch.

"Thank you, but no. I'm fine," answered the man.

"Well, then, let's get down to business. How can we help you?"

"We are not prepared for war. We need the advice of your War Department. Our hope is that the Confederation can bring this situation to an end, quickly, and with as few casualties as possible. We have tried diplomacy. In talks, we have discovered Xanadu feels entitled to take over the curbite mines. They realize how valuable curbite is and are greedy. Unexplainably, they want all of it. This is not reasonable They feel the rest of the Confederation has used enough. They want to control it under a new confederation."

The President absorbed the Ambassador's words and replied, "Of course. I will present your re*Quest*s to Congress, but I feel certain you shall have our aid. Whatever you need. The Colonial Solar Confederation is the legitimate ruling body of the thirteen colonies. You are our allies. We will provide you with defenses, aircraft and any other means you need to bring this civil war to an end."

"Thank you, Mr. President. My secretary has prepared our requests in writing. I look forward to a positive response from Congress."

On the Ambassador's cue, everyone stood. They shook hands while one of Dan's aides motioned them to follow him to the room's entrance.

One of the aides walked up to Dan. "We'll get right on this, Mr. President. You have fifteen minutes before you need to be in the Press Room to give your update on the Impact Recovery Effort."

"All right. Thanks. Just give me a few minutes."

"Of course, Mr. President," answered the aide as he closed the door behind him.

Dan sat at his desk, lifted his head to the ceiling and closed his eyes. He should look over his address to the reporters, but his mind couldn't get off the crisis among the thirteen colonies. Could it be resolved quickly or would it escalate? What did it mean for Earth? Giving the Confederation arms put the Earth in danger.

After a few minutes a knock disturbed his thoughts.

"Come in."

"It's time, Mr. President."

"Thanks. I'll be right there." Dan stood and collected his thoughts. He focused on the moment and headed to the Press Room where he would explain to the public how the Earth had made great strides in recovering from the asteroid impact two and a half years ago.

As he entered the Press Room he smiled. In the next day or two he would address the nation about war in the colonies. But not today. He stepped up to the podium.

"Good morning. We gather today to update you on the great strides we have made in our Recovery Program…"

CHAPTER 58
Jonathan & Rihanna Commissioned

Tuesday, November 4, 2061, 1:20 p.m., Correll, Moon

"That was a delicious lunch, Rihanna."

"Thank you, Joe," she said to her father-in-law. "I know you love apple dumplings. They make a meal, don't they?"

"Where did you get the apples? Joe inquired. "I haven't had one in years."

"A cargo ship comes from Earth every week. We get fresh produce and other supplies from them. That's one benefit to being so close to Earth. They're still good when they get here."

"Well. That tasted great. Let me help you clean up. Then we need to get busy with why the Confederation appointed me to come here."

Jonathan interceded. "We can talk in the living room. Rex, the robot, will take care of the kitchen. He's been a great help to Rihanna. Our only problem having him has been Rune asks him the answers to his homework *Quest*ions, so I modified his computer brain, so Rune can't do that anymore." Laughing, they moved to the living room.

"Where is my grandson, today?" They all sat down.

"He is at school and won't be home for two hours. Believe it or not, I take him to work and he helps me in my laboratory. They say he's a genius at computers. I am hoping he'll help me with my project someday, if I don't complete it before then. Since money is tight, it'll probably take until he's older for me to finish it."

Joe's smile disappeared. "Are you talking about the Oneida Project?"

Jonathan frowned. "How did you know about that?"

"I know many things, Jonathan."

"How much do you know?" reiterated the astounded son.

"I am a member of the ten-man Security Council of the Confederation. You are working on your Oneida Project that will download memories from a human brain into a computer, making the person immortal. Our intelligence unit has been keeping track of your progress. We have learned that you are very close to accomplishing your objective, but are running into financial problems. This is one reason I am here. If you agree, the Confederation will help you in this area, and we will become partners."

"Why would they do this?"

"Since the War began, we have learned Xanadu is working on a secret mutant bacteria that could kill the human race. They are counting on a vaccine to give to their people to make them immune to the effects of this lethal bacterial strain. If you succeed in your Oneida Project, we will be assured that the Confederation will survive, because we will become androids and impervious to their endeavors to destroy us."

Jonathan stared at his father. "It has been my life's dream to create such an android. With the help of curbite I am almost there. I do need a sponsor to supply the funds to complete my prototype. My impetus to finish has been to enable mankind to travel to the outer reaches of the galaxy. To save the human race from extinction is a greater stimulus to finish my project. I would be honored to be part of this effort."

Joe turned to Rihanna. "I also have a Commission for you. We have reason to believe that Xanadu is experimenting with the genetically-altered bacteria, sterococcus. We will supply you with this dangerous bacteria in hopes you can find a drug providing immunity to it before Xanadu does. Commissioning you and Jonathan gives us two possible solutions to this threat. What do you think?"

Jonathan observed Rihanna's reaction. She put her hand to her chin and gazed at him. It would be dangerous work. One mishap in the lab and death would result. But he knew she had to accept the request. She was the most qualified physician and scientist in all the colonies in the area of genetics and pathogenic engineering.

She turned back to Joe. "Of course I'll join the team. I must do what is right. There is no doubt if Xanadu discovers a vaccine they would not hesitate to use the sterococcus bacteria on the rest of us. With all of us dead, they would rule the cosmos."

With fear and admiration, Jonathan turned to his father. "When do these Commissions take effect?"

"Immediately. I will stay long enough for you to read the contracts and sign them. The funds will be deposited in your company's account. The Confederation is anxious for your answers."

"I will need a couple of days to read them and have Paul, my lawyer to look them over, if that's O.K."

"Of course. This will give me time to spend time with my grandson. It's about time for him to get home, isn't it?"

"Pretty soon. Can I get you a cup of tea?"

The meeting ended. Jonathan chatted Joe about the more mundane happenings on Mars. They conversed for an hour and sipped tea, waiting for Rune to get home from the university.

Suddenly the door burst open, and Rune skipped in, running immediately to his grandfather and gave him a big hug. "Thank you, Pops, for my new star tracker. I love it!"

"I'm glad you received it in one piece. I hope you had a wonderful birthday."

"I had a party. Some of my friends came over, and we played games and ate cake. I wish you could have been here."

Joe eyed Jonathan and turned back to his grandson. "It's a little hard to travel these days, with the war going on, but I'm here now."

"Oh that's all right, Pops," Rune returned. "Do you want to go to my room and see the other presents I got?"

Joe winked at Jonathan. "Oh, yes," answered the old man. "I'd love to."

When the two were gone, Jonathan went over to his wife, leaning down to hug her. "It'll be all right. Either you or I will come up with a solution to stop Xanadu from harming us."

He stared over her shoulder at the wall. Now, I have to convince myself. He heard laughter come from the Rune's room. If not for Rihanna or me, we must do it for Rune.

CHAPTER 59
Rune Reborn

Monday, October 10, 2063, 9:08 a.m., Correll, Moon

"Jonathan, I'm afraid."

"Don't be. It may be his only chance for survival."

"But any day now I could find the vaccine."

Rihanna moved to the window and stared outside."

"Rihanna, it's been two years. Xanadu could release the bacteria any day. If they do, we'll all be dead."

"I know. I know. But Rune's our son. What if something goes wrong?"

Jonathan stood and put his arms around the distraught woman. "Two hundred and forty-three people are now androids. My work is a success. If we download Rune's memories into a computerized brain, and give him a new body, he will live indefinitely. We can download ourselves later when curbite isn't so scarce. Right now, Xanadu has the upper hand. They control the Ceres mine, and Europa. They will soon overtake Mars. If they do that, the war is lost. It is good Dad didn't live to see this all happen."

Rihanna turned around and hugged Jonathan. "You're right. And I'm so sorry about your Dad's fatal heart attack. I know you still grieve. His lonely heart couldn't take it anymore. I don't think he ever got over your mom's death."

"You're right. He never remarried. But now we have to think of the future. Rune is our future. He will be part of the future of the *Homo Sapiens* species."

"Why do you say that?"

"I have some news to tell you. It is top secret, but you are cleared to know."

"What?"

"The Confederation is working on a new program. It is called the Grand Exodus Project, and should be ready by next year."

"Go on." Rihanna wrung her hands in anticipation of what Jonathan was about to say.

"Earth is secretly building three starships, the *Ninã*, the *Pinta*, and the *Santa Maria*. A new propulsion system has been developed using Dark Energy that will propel the human race into space outside of our Solar System. Astronomers have discovered a planet similar to ours named Gliese 351e, situated about twenty and a half light years away. The Confederation believes we must send our most promising and elite crew in the form of androids, to form a colony outside of our Solar System. We are afraid if we don't, the human species may be doomed to extinction."

"Who will go?"

"A list is being drafted. The best minds in many areas will be chosen."

"And does this list include us?"

"Yes."

"And Rune?"

"Yes."

Rihanna turned again to peer out the window. "But I am so close to finding a vaccine. We could die, anyway, outside the Solar System."

Jonathan furrowed his eyebrows. "Not if we are androids."

Rihanna spun around to face her husband. "I'm not sure I want to be an android. I'm not sure I want to leave the Moon. This is home." Tears rolled down her face.

Jonathan knew his wife did not like change. He could not believe it when she said she would accept a position on the Moon. But they were younger, then. After several years, Correll was home like she said. But life changed.

He had more news.

"Rihanna. Come over and sit down. I have more to tell you."

"Oh, please," pleaded Rihanna. "Not more bad news."

"I am afraid so. Our intelligence believes Xanadu has developed the vaccine for the deadly sterococcus bacteria, and could begin to inoculate its own people immediately. It is believed they are using another rare, genetically altered bacteria, only found on the asteroid, Ida, that kills the sterococcus bacteria. When their people are all vaccinated, they will release the lethal organism to the rest of the Solar System including Earth. You do not have much time. Only your team of scientists have the means to find these rare bacteria. The Confederation wants you to go to Ida and harvest it. It may be our only hope."

"Will you go with me?"

"No, darling. I have work to do here."

"Please. I want you to go." Rihanna pleaded.

"Who will take care of Rune?" Jonathan countered.

"Rex and my parents will take care of Rune. Please. We shouldn't be gone long."

"We don't know that. But OK. I'll go with you under one condition."

"What is that?"

"I download Rune's memories and brain contents into a robot I made especially for him. If his physical body is harmed, he will live on through his android."

"All right. You win. When will you do the transfer?"

"Tonight. We must leave for Ida, tomorrow."

****

"Doctor Cooper? What are you doing here so late, to-night? Hello, Mrs. Cooper. How are you, Rune? The three walked past the security guard and made their way to Jona-than's lab.

"Can I play on the supercomputer?" implored Rune.

"Not tonight, my son." Joe used his imprint code to en-ter the laboratory and turned on the lights. He walked over to the robot closet and retrieved Ralph, his robot assistant.

"Good evening, Doctor. How may I assist you?"

"Ralph, we're going to give Rune some happy juice. Would you get it ready?"

"Right away, Doctor Cooper." The robot went to the cupboard and began preparing a sedative to relax and partial-ly sedate Rune.

"Come with me, Rune. I want to show you something." Rihanna sat down on a stool. They walked down a short hallway and entered another room full of doors. Jonathan stopped in front of one and used a special code to open it.

Rune gasped. There in the closet stood a robot. "It looks just like me! Is it mine?"

"It will be, Rune."

Jonathan pressed buttons on the waist of the Rune look-a-like robot, and the machine began to move.

"Cool!" shouted Rune.

Jonathan addressed the robot. "Follow us, 706."

"Yes, sir," said the robot as he began to move out of the closet.

"He sounds just like me. I love him, Dad." Rune took the robot's hand as they made their way back to where Rihanna waited for them."

Ralph walked over to Rune and held out a vessel of blue liquid. "This is for you, Rune. You need to hop on the that table and lay down."

"Why does he want me to do that, Dad?"

"Because the happy juice will make you feel sleepy and I don't want you to fall down."

Obediently, Rune climbed onto the table and sat on the side sipping his drink. When he had finished, his eyelids began to close, and Rihanna gently lifted his legs onto the table until he reclined.

Ralph and Jonathan, immediately, began to connect probes to Rune's head. The other ends were attached to a machine. Extensions on the other end of the apparatus connected to Rune's look-a-like robot.

"Have you checked everything?" Jonathan asked Ralph.

"Yes. We're ready to flip the switch."

"Then, let's do it."

Ralph connected the relay. Lights on the machine indicated the transfer was taking place. For several minutes nothing moved. When four minutes and twenty-two seconds passed, the robot's eyes opened. Without moving, 706 scanned the other beings in the room.

After five minutes and thirty-two seconds, the new android spoke. "Hi, Dad."

Although Jonathan had witnessed over two-hundred transformations, this announcement by the android sent shivers up his spine. "Hi, Son."

All the indicators on the transfer machine emitted green lights. The process was complete. Rune now had a body-double that would long out live his carbon-based life form. If Rune periodically updated this android, there would be no gaps in his memories. As he grew older, he could be down-loaded again into another appropriate body. If injured, parts could be replaced. Rune had become immortal.

Except for one nano-transmitter in his android's brain. Jonathan could not completely eliminate this minute flaw, that, if injured, could kill the android. But the chances of this were several million to one.

After taking Rune's double back to the closet and shutting him down, Jonathan scooped Rune, sleeping, off the operating table and carried him to the waiting vehicle.

At home, with Rune safely tucked into bed for the night, Rihanna and Jonathan kissed him and shut his bedroom door.

After packing for the trip, Jonathan lay in bed and prayed. He knew Ida held many dangers. The Titans of Xanadu roamed the asteroid. Although thirty-five by four-teen miles in size, it would be difficult to mine Ida undetect-ed. Hopefully, Rihanna's team of eight scientists could get in and out quickly. Would there be enough time?

CHAPTER 60
Ida

Wednesday, December 4, 2074, 3:32 p.m., asteroid Ida

"Watch your step," the commander of the mission said to Rihanna as she stepped down off the small starship used to transport them to the asteroid, Ida.

Rihanna had not worn a spacesuit in many years, and felt awkward and clumsy in the attire. The craft had settled down on the barren hunk of nickel in a valley thought by Rihanna's scientists to have the best chance to uncover and scoop up the necessary bacteria.

"Thanks," she replied to Commander Luke. "I think I will dig over there."

Jonathan stayed inside the spacecraft and monitored the events that took place outside on a screen. Rihanna turned and waved at the starship, knowing her husband saw her in the lit up area around the landing site. She moved to the desired location with the commander and one other scientist. When she scanned the area with her light, the ground appeared disturbed. Is this the same place the Xanadu scientists had dug? It gave her the creeps to think these killers had been here. But, on the other hand, perhaps buried in this location existed the bacteria they had come to find. She bent over and scooped up dirt and filled a bag attached to her side.

"I think we have enough," she announced to the two with her.

"Good. Let's go before we're spotted. Judging by these other footprints, we aren't the first to have been here."

Rihanna stashed her small shovel and began hopping toward the starship. The lights from the vehicle guided her. She raised her head to the starlit night. It was then that out of her peripheral vision she thought she saw another light. I must be imagining things.

"Luke. Do you see a light over there to the right? It's getting bigger."

The commander and the other scientist, Leah, both agreed at the same time.

"Titans!"

A hundred yards separated them from the safety of the starship. Rihanna thought her lungs would burst as she hopped frantically toward their ride home. As they shone their lights in the direction of the oncoming beam, they made out a ground rover speeding to their location.

"They're intercepting us!" shouted Luke.

It became clear they couldn't make it to the starship. Rihanna gasped as the rover pulled up beside them. Two men jumped out. She put her hand on the shovel thinking she could use it as a weapon. As she tried to raise the shovel she felt a sting on her arm. The weapon, used by one of the Titans pierced through the spacesuit. Rihanna dropped to the ground.

Inside the starcraft, Jonathan watched for a sign of his wife. And then he saw the light. But there should be three lights. And it came too fast. He alerted the other scientists and they gazed out the two-foot square portal.

"It must be the Xanadu, Titans!" yelled Jonathan. Although the starship did not carry arms, each scientist had a laser gun. And the Titans should not be able to penetrate their hatch.

Jonathan feared for Rihanna. Hopefully, the evil inhabitants of the rover did not see her party. He hastily went to the radio transmitter and sent a S.O.S. message to Vesta, the closest colony. Help could not be there for at least a day. And where were the rest of the Titans? Their starship must be somewhere close.

"What if they breach our hatch?" one of the remaining scientists asked.

"We're dead meat," answered one of the others.

They could now make out the vehicle carrying two men wielding laser rifles. They drove up to the starship and stopped. The two men jumped off the rover and fired their rifles at the hatch. Jonathan heard a ping sound, but the door stayed secure. One of the men hopped back to the rover and pulled out a small case. He made his way to the hatch and set the box near the entrance. They moved back to the rover and drove some distance away.

Behind them, the box exploded. The lights on the starship went black and a gaping hole killed the occupants, instantly. The two murderers drove over the ridge where their mother ship waited for their return.

CHAPTER 61
Survivor

Tuesday, September 5, 2064, 6:00 p.m., Correll, Moon

"Rune Joseph Cooper, it's time to blow out your candles," laughed Rihanna's Dad. Rune ran around the table chasing his friend, George.

"OK, Papa." Rune stopped and sat down at the table. The twelve people attending his birthday party began to sing, Happy Birthday. When they were finished, Rune took in a deep breath and blew out all eleven candles.

While cake and ice cream were passed out, Dr. Rice walked up to Rune's grandfather. "Can I have a private word with you before I need to go?"

"Of course. We can go in my room."

Once in the bedroom, Dr. Rice, the new head of Cooper Industries, sat down on a settee by the window. "We need to talk about Rune. I don't know how much Jonathan and Rihanna told you, but Rune is a very special young man. Can you come to my office tomorrow? There is much you need to know. I have obtained a security clearance for you and Mrs. Rand."

"Of course. We will be there."

****

The next morning, Rune's grandparents, made their way to Dr. Rice's office.

"Good morning. Come on in," said the cordial man.

"Would you like some coffee?"

"No thank you."

"All right. Well, let's start. As I said yesterday, Rune is a special boy. He excels in school so much that he could graduate this year and enter college next fall. His expertise is computer technology. His goal is to make a computer that does everything. Pretty lofty, don't you think?

As you know, from the news, Xanadu has released the deadly sterococcus bacteria. Rihanna's lab has finally found a vaccine that keeps us alive, but has deemed us all sterile. We are calling the war with the Titans 'The Blood War,' because when we all grow old and die, it will be the end of blood humans. The only *Homo sapiens* who will survive, indefinitely, will be the ones whose minds have been downloaded into an android.

Jonathan's company, Cooper Industries, has been commissioned by the Confederation, to download the brains of select citizens who have been chosen to leave this Solar System to travel to another unspoiled planet named Gliese.

Rune has been chosen to be part of The Exodus Project. Three starships are completed, and will depart by the end of the year. Rihanna and Jonathan were supposed to be part of this venture. Since the Titans have been defeated, thanks to the aid from Earth, the remaining humans can live out their lives in peace. But there will be no children unless a discovery is made and the outcome is reversed."

Jacob and Mabel Rand said nothing for a few moments. Finally, Rune's grandfather said, "That's a lot to take in. I'm sorry, but I'm a little overwhelmed. I know Rune loves computers and programming. But how does this all work? Downloading his brain and all?"

Dr. Rice continued, "Jonathan downloaded Rune's brain-scan and memories into an android the night before he and Rihanna left for Ida. The likeness to Rune would be part of The Exodus Project and would leave in four months. The organic Rune will stay with you and live out his normal life. Since he has taken the vaccine, as we all have, he cannot procreate. When his generation dies, it will be the end of humans as we know them, unless a reversal is found, which is unlikely. Intelligence indicates that the people of Xanadu can't have children, either. There has been talk of cloning, but nothing has been decided.

"As the biological guardians of Rune, you will not want for anything. Rune is a billionaire with his trust from his grandfather and his inheritance from his parents."

Jacob felt relieved. The furrows on his forehead softened and he smiled. "Thank the heavens, Rune will stay with us." Mabel nodded.

"Yes, well, we'll keep in touch. We need to introduce Rune to the computers on board the *Ninã*, which is the starship he has been assigned to. In addition, he'll need training before his android double departs. His memories will be downloaded for the last time the night before the three starships begin their voyage. We want Rune, the Android, to have as many memories as possible before he departs the Moon for Gliese.

****

Back at home, Papa and Nana waited for Rune to get home from school. At three-thirty Rune walked into the house and went straight to the refrigerator. "Anything good to eat? I'm starving!"

"Rune, we need to talk to you. There are some plans for you that you need to know about."

"What plans?" he questioned while he ate a big hunk of Gouda cheese.

"Come sit at the table."

Rune's eyes moved from his Papa to his Nana. "Sounds serious." He sat down.

"It's our understanding that you know an android made in your image exists at the laboratory? The time has come for it to be used for a voyage out of our Solar System.

When it leaves, its brain will be a duplicate of yours with all your memories and brain make-up. In a sense, you will live on past your lifetime in the form of an android. Does this make any sense?"

Rune's eyes were as big as saucers. "That's cool!"

His grandparents looked briefly at each other and smiled. The hard part appeared to be over. Papa continued. "You will receive training for the expedition, and it will be downloaded into the brain of the android the night before the starship departs on its journey."

"Sounds like fun," replied Rune. "Do you know what I will have to learn?"

"Yes. You will study the main computer that will control the starship. The crew will use your expertise."

"Wow. That's flattering. When's dinner?"

"In an hour," replied Nana. "Now, you need to do your homework."

"I've done it. Can I go to George's house?"

"Sure, just be back for supper at five o'clock."

Rune headed toward the door. "Don't worry. I won't miss a meal."

When he had gone, Nana said, "That went well."

Papa stared at the door. The implications of Rune existing in two places at one time overwhelmed him. But it meant that the human species would live on in another part of the galaxy.

He turned to his wife and said, "Yes it did." It felt good to know that the memory of Rune's family would live on forever, even if it existed in a non-carbon form."

Perhaps there is hope for the human race.

CHAPTER 62
Preparation

Monday, September 18, 2064, 7:20 a.m., Earth

"Man, this starship is huge!" Rune shouted as he boarded the *Ninã*.

"Yes. It's three-hundred and twenty-two-feet long. This will be your android's home for a long time."

"How long?"

Rune's guardian and guide answered, "Hundreds to thousands of years, possibly, until we land on Gliese and make a new home. I am sorry your mom and dad aren't also going."

Rune tried not to think about living without his mom and dad. He pretended they were coming back some day. He winced.

"Thank you. I wish they were, too. Could you show me the rest of the starship?"

Rune's guide cleared his throat. He knew it was a sensitive subject for the eleven-year old. "Of course. I want to show you where your quarters will be. And then we'll go to the control rooms where the main computers are located. You will get your chance, during the voyage, to do programming and upgrading of our computer systems. I understand you want to build a super computer?"

"Yes. Computers are my area of interest. I plan to make them my life's work. It would be nice to know time will be unlimited."

They walked along a window-less corridor that Rune thought stretched forever. After many turns, he was totally lost. It would take a long time to learn his way around the vast starship. Finally, they stopped at two double doors that opened with little sound as they approached. After passing several more doors, they stopped, and the guide put a code on the numbered pad located to the left of the portal in front of them. He noticed the room number eighty-six printed on the door as they entered.

The sleeping room appeared to be about twelve-feet square. A bunk-size bed and desk with a chair made up the furniture. On the wall hung a computer monitor.

"This is your private sleeping area. The rest of the starship is public access. You will come here to have time to sleep and be by yourself. An adult supervisor will be assigned to you to help you adjust. Do you have any *Quest*ions so far?"

"Yes. When are we going to the computer room?"

"Right now, if you want to."

"Let's go." Rune headed for the door.

On the way, the guide pointed out social centers where inhabitants would gather, kitchens and dining areas.

After about five minutes, the guide said, "Here we are," and opened another door that exposed a thirty-square-feet area. Monitors filled the walls. Tables expanded along the perimeter with stations every few feet where the programmers, technicians and Rune would labor with touch-keyboards to control the inner workings of the starship. Computer processors based on stands under which contained shelves filled with tools and computer parts filled the center of the room.

"Now, this is where I will spend my time. Is one of these stations mine?"

"I am sure one will be assigned to you."

"That's great." Rune beamed.

"It's time to get you back to your hotel. Tomorrow, you travel back home to the Moon."

Outside, Rune scanned the base. "Where are the other two starships?"

"They are in specially built hangars."

"Will they be taking off the same time as the *Ninã*?"

"Yes. You will all be together, to aid each other on your journey, if necessary. They will come to Correll when the time is ready for all the androids to board."

On the way back to the hotel, Rune pondered the prospect of being in two places at once. He had learned in his training, his organic body would be at home with his grandparents and he would live out his life, in the flesh, on the Moon. But somewhere in the Cosmos, his android would exist, and outlive his mortal body while exploring outer space.

Weird, he told himself.

CHAPTER 63
The Last Download

Sunday, December 24, 2064, 8:00 a.m., Correll, Moon

"Are you ready for your last visit?"

"I'm ready," Rune exclaimed smiling.

Papa and Rune entered the rover and were transported to Cooper Industries where the boy's android waited for the last and final entry of Rune's memories into its database.

"Are you sure he will remember everything?"

"Yes, Rune. He has learned your whole family's history clear back to your great-grandparents. He'll know more than you about the history of the human race. There are stored databases in the mainframe of the supercomputer on board the *Ninã* that your android will learn about. There will be plenty of time. It will take beyond our lifetimes to arrive to the planet, Gliese. Of course they will be looking for short cuts to get there. It should be very exciting.

"I wish I could go."

"It is too dangerous to try to go in our present carbon-based form. And it's too far. Besides, in a way, you are going in the form of Rune, the Android. He looks, thinks, acts and feels like you."

They arrived at the laboratory. Other chosen people stood in line as their identifications were verified. When completed, each person was led to different rooms to have their memories and brain makeup downloaded.

A girl about his age stood in front of him. Although not yet interested in girls, this one he thought was beautiful. She smiled at him as her mother, called "Come on Lore."

Once again, Rune went through the procedure. This time, familiar with the painless transfer, he opted to stay awake. Since there did not involve a sedative application, he finished in fifteen minutes.

He jumped off the table and hugged his android.

"I will always remember you," the android blurted.

A tear came to Rune's eye. "And I'll remember you. Don't tell any of my secrets."

The android winked at his counterpart. "Of course not."

Papa asked the android, "When do you leave?"

"Tomorrow."

"Well, then, I guess this is goodbye. I wish you a safe journey." Papa shook the android's hand.

"Come on Rune, we are going to meet your grandmother and have breakfast."

"Good bye, Rune," the android said as they headed for the door.

Rune turned around and was amazed at how much his android resembled himself. It was like peering into a mirror. "Good bye, Rune," said the real boy. "Have fun in the Cosmos."

The android answered, "You will always be in my thoughts. At this moment we become two since I am now activated and am basically "alive." We will now have separate memories, but you will always be with me."

Rune and Papa shut the door and walked back to the rover. Rune knew the android would outlive him. His heart ached with longing to explore the universe. But he knew it wouldn't happen. By blood, he was bound to the Moon and the Solar System. He was bound to the now. His android represented the future of mankind.

They stopped in front of the restaurant. "What are you going to eat, Rune?"

"I think I'll have a big stack of pancakes."

****

In the lab, Dr. Rice gave the android, Rune, his final instructions. "Rune, you have learned your lessons well. You are ready to board the *Niñã*. The three starships have landed outside of Correll. At noon, today, you and three-hundred other androids will begin boarding the three starships. You will take Robert, your dad's robot with you to watch over you and keep you company. We will leave from here on buses. Your journey is scheduled for a six a.m. departure tomorrow morning. Do you have any questions?

"No. I am programmed to be activated at four a.m. tomorrow morning. I will be ready for the initiation of the Exodus Project."

CHAPTER 64
The Exodus Project Unfolds

Monday, December 25, 2064, 5:00 a.m., Correll, Moon

At five a.m. android, Rune, and Robert, boarded his new home, the starship *Nina*, along with ninety-nine other crewmembers. The other two-hundred, bloodless androids boarded the *Pinta* and the *Santa Maria*. Each android, an expert in a necessary field, would be a contributor to The Exodus Project. Among the group were doctors, scientists, engineers, and others whose minds had been compiled from their biological counterparts left behind to live out their lives on a dying Solar System.

With the layout of the starship programmed in his brain, Rune quickly made his way to the computer area. Robert stayed in his room. He walked around from station to station and there on one desk a nameplate, with "Rune" inscribed on it, marked the area assigned to him. Pleased, and eager, he sat down and pressed the button to start up his computer. He inserted his identification code and after a few seconds, the machine said, "Hello, Rune. Welcome to the *Niñã*."

Excited, he entered, "What shall I call you?"

"You must give me a name," answered the machine.

Rune thought for a minute, and then as he smiled he entered, "I will call you "Mother.""

At 5:55 a.m. an announcement alerted Rune and the rest of the starship, that in five minutes the fleet would lift off.

Eagerly, Rune made his way to the observation deck. He gazed out the thirty-foot-wide window at the Moon landscape along with many others. Robots hustled to clear the area for their take off. The *Pinta* and the *Santa Maria* gleamed dark orange, the color of curbite, as their entryways were secured. At precisely 6:00 a.m., Rune heard the hum of the engines revving up as they slowly lifted off the Moon's surface.

Within seconds, the Moon reduced in size and appeared a marble in the dark sky. The Earth, blue, green and white, shrunk smaller and smaller.

Armed with the memories of the Earth, Moon, his parents and grandparents, and his brief eleven-year history in the Solar System, Rune began his new life's adventure.

The Exodus Project had begun.

THE END

Excerpt from
THE EXODUS PROJECT
Book Two of the Exodus Trilogy

CHAPTER ONE
Starship Lost

"Where are you going in such a hurry, Rune?"

"I don't have time to talk, Rusty. Didn't you hear the alarm?" Rune ran past his best friend.

"They're always a drill," shouted the man as he watched his sprinting buddy disappear around the bend of a corridor in the starship, *Niña*. Rusty ignored the warning alarm.

Rune rushed into the computer room, green eyes scanning the screens covering the walls. His head stopped at the screen nicknamed "the window." The three-foot by four-foot display showed the image from a camera placed on the nose of the starcraft. He opened his mouth, and dropped his jaw at what he saw. They were hurling toward an unexplainable, glowing ring with a black center. Around it, stars dotted the sky, twinkling like normal. His six-foot-eight body dropped into a chair.

The science and computer genius blurted, "Mother! Do you hear me? What's going on?"

The supercomputer responded instantly, "The phenomenon in the path of the *Niña*, is what Earth's physicists have theorized as a wormhole or shortcut through spacetime. Stable versions of such wormholes have been suggested as dark matter candidates. Small wormholes, held open by a negative-mass cosmic string, were inflated to macroscopic size by cosmic inflation during the Big Bang."

"What? We don't know if such a thing exists. Are you sure?"

Mother sounded indignant. "Have I ever been wrong before?"

"Rune?" A voice from the room's intercom interrupted. A flashing button on his console indicated it came from the bridge.

"Yes, Captain Reynolds?" answered Rune to the familiar voice.

The captain spoke with urgency. "Are you getting any strange outputs from Mother?"

"Yes, as a matter-of-fact. She is saying we are approaching a phenomenon known as a theoretical wormhole. We didn't know they existed. Scientists have never observed one. If we traverse this warped space-time, we could end up in another part of the universe, or at least, the galaxy."

"I agree," replied the captain. "Let's get out of here!"

Rune stared at the starship's systems monitor displaying the captain's inputs into the controls. The performance indicated the captain struggled to perform a 180 degree turn. The displays were erratic. But as the heading changed, the rate of turn slowed. When it reached 90-degrees, it stopped all together. The *Niña* was being swallowed down the throat of the wormhole sideways, AND the vessel was accelerating!

The captain shouted, "It's no use. We don't have the power to break free!"

The starship began to shutter as it reeled out of control. Rune grabbed the desk to keep his chair from moving. He saw Rusty wobble into the room his wide brown eyes staring back. His face flamed red as his hair. His knuckles were white as he held on for dear life to the bolted desks and clunked down into his own chair. Blackness engulfed the vessel as they hurled into the unknown.

Maybe Mother's right as usual, thought Rune. She's never been wrong before. *Were they waiting to be crushed and stretched into oblivion? Or would they survive the wormhole?*

"Mother, what makes you think we are entering a wormhole?" he managed to say with not much more than a whisper.

Mother spoke in a calm female voice. "Wormholes exist in many sizes. The one in our proximity appears to fit the mathematical description using electromagnetic field energy. Some compare them to black holes, but they are not the same. My calculations indicate the curbite, making up everything in this starship, including your bodies and me, will withstand the negative forces being exerted. We will survive the entry, and transport to another part of the galaxy. The exotic matter used to fortify our shields will protect us. We will not be crushed."

Rune raised his eyebrows. "Are you sure?" he questioned. "The vibration is growing worse. If you are correct, and you always are, this is a first."

With a shaking finger, he pressed the button linking him to the bridge. Captain Reynolds answered immediately. "What is Mother indicating?"

Rune turned his head back and forth scanning the screens, "We need to hold on, but it appears we're safe. However, we may end up in another part of the galaxy."

"Where?"

"She doesn't know, yet. It's like a wrinkle in space-time. We can't control where we end up. Have you notified the *Pinta* and the *Santa Maria*? They are only one day's time behind us."

"They aren't replying to my transmissions." The captain sounded distraught.

"Can you send a Red Alert, using a series of intense radio signals?" offered Rune.

"I've tried. But I am receiving no response. The black hole is warping our communications capability."

Indicated by the starship's clock, the vibration continued for several seconds.

Rune thought about their trip up until now. They had been traveling toward an Earth-like planet, Gliese 581 g, in the Constellation Libra, for eight years, using calculations derived from their starship's Earth-based time. Thrust to near the speed of light, the starship's occupants expected to reach their anticipated new home in twelve more years. Having left the doomed Solar System, the emigrants' mission encompassed a trek to this "new" Earth. Memories of their former human-selves had been downloaded into their newly formed curbite brains. Their human counterparts, infected with disease during biological warfare, rendered them sterile. They would live out their generation and become extinct. To avoid this bleak conclusion, three-hundred-humans, chosen for their various gifts and expertise, became androids and joined together on three starships in search of Gliese 581 g.

Now, that hope could be gone.

Rune turned and faced the machine in the middle of the room. He thought about how close he had become to the ten-foot by twelve-foot supercomputer. He named her Mother in honor of his own biological parents, killed in the Blood Wars nine years ago. His mom and dad, physicians, sought a remedy to reverse the sterilizing effects of bacteria released by the evil Titans of Xanadu. While on Ida, Titans attacked and murdered them, rendering the human race doomed to extinction.

Rune, a computer genius and inventor of many of her systems, seldom left the room where monitors indicated Mother's functions. An unmade, folding, portable bed sat in the corner. Three other techs, including his friend, Rusty, helped him keep her working. Mother maintained the starship's many functions and constantly updated the simpler computers to keep them running smoothly. Now, who knew where they were headed? Mother, alone, would do her calculations.

The clock on the wall indicated eight minutes had passed. *Could the vibration be slowing down?* He checked the window monitor. *Was he seeing stars?* The chair stopped dancing. The vibrations trickled to a stop. A few more seconds and the starship returned to gliding smoothly through space. The faint hum of the negative energy engines sounded normal once again. It was over. And, they were alive!

Rune stared at the monitor in front of him, anxiously waiting for Mother to complete her calculations. All of the starship's systems displayed normal readings.

An announcement over the starship's intercom noted the "all clear" to all occupants of the vessel.

Once again, Captain Reynolds chimed the computer room. "Rune, has Mother given you any other information? My navigational system needs new input. I cannot get a read on where we are."

"No, sir," replied Rune. "I'm also waiting. She has not spoken for several minutes. I'll call you as soon as she recalculates our position."

Rune glanced at the window, and turned his attention back to the supercomputer. "Mother do you have any information?"

"Yes. My indications tell me we have transported to the constellation Virgo, near the star Spica. This celestial body is five times the size of the Earth's sun and has at least twenty planets orbiting around it. I will give Captain Reynolds the coordinates for one that appears to be Earth-like in size and distance from Spica. It may be habitable for your species."

Rune scratched his head. Eyes wide, his hands settled under his chin. "Virgo. That's light years away from where we were. What happened? Can you tell me?"

"Yes. Based on my readings going through this wormhole, the metal curbite and the exotic matter making up our ship and protective system enabled us to travel through it without any ill effects. I suggest you use them in the future to navigate through the universe. It is probable millions of wormholes exist throughout the cosmos. Using my new data, I have been able to map the locations of some of them and have entered the coordinates into my memory banks."

This discovery is marvelous. Travel through the universe would be changed forever. He notified the captain.

"Sir, I have astounding news. We traversed a wormhole. Can you believe it? They are real. Scientists speculated on them for centuries, but there was no proof. Mother is currently mapping the locations of the ones close by so we won't accidentally fall into one, again."

"That's great news, Rune. But we were on our way to Gliese 581g. Mother has given me new coordinates on my instruments. Can it be true we are near the star Spica?"

"That's what she is saying. There is an unnamed planet that has possibilities for life forms not too far away. You can request the navigational input from Mother to travel there instead of Gliese 581g."

"I think considering where we are, we don't have another option."

"Have you heard from the other ships?" Rune asked.

"No. We are still sending signals. Ask Mother if it is possible they missed the wormhole. Maybe she knows."

Rune inquired, "Mother, do you know the location of the other two starships?"

"Yes," answered the supercomputer. "They are on their original course to Gliese 581g. "

We must send them a message. But it will take light years for the other two starships to receive it—unless Mother can contact them, somehow. How does she know where they are? Mother learns exponentially. In eight years she has surpassed all the other computers combined. The crew thinks I am a genius, but no one can compare to Mother.

Rune's shoulders drooped in dismay and disappointment. *Would they ever join together, again? Or are they all on their own?*

ABOUT THE AUTHOR

Pat McAnulty grew up in Jamestown, N.Y. during the "happy days" of the fifties and sixties. As a child she loved writing in her journals. In high school she wrote stories and poems for the school paper.

In 1972 she and her husband, Jim, took flying lessons, and she went on to graduate from Embry Riddle Aeronautical University's Flight Technology Program. While her four children were small McAnulty worked as a flight instructor. Eventually she was hired by Piedmont Airlines and then US Airways after the two airlines merged.

After she retired from flying, Pat returned to her love of writing. Today she lives with her husband and her dog, Rosie, in Fort Myers where she enjoys writing and spending time with her family. A critique group called The Scribblers gave her the groundwork to write a trilogy of science fiction novels – The Beginning- Book One of the Exodus Trilogy is her first novel.